SHEYANNE WARREN

Sorcery & Suspicious Shenanigans

A Deceptive High Novel

Trigger Warning:

This novel contains references to grief, parental loss, emotional trauma, bullying, and systemic injustice, as well as fantasy violence and combat-related injuries. Reader discretion is advised.

First edition

ISBN: 979-8-9856989-7-8

Editing by Shelley Lopez

This book was professionally typeset on Reedsy.
Find out more at reedsy.com

Contents

I

From The Garden to Deceptive High

Can't Stop, Won't Gasp

Lanelle Sparks dove into the water. Not breaking the surface, she swam as fast as she could. Her lungs started to burn, but she pushed herself. She wanted to see how long she could last with one breath.

If she could make it the length of the pool with only one breath, she would be unstoppable in competition.

Her burning lungs were becoming unbearable. She slowed a little. It felt like she had to switch her concentration from speed to not inhaling water. When she couldn't take it anymore, she popped up for air. Her lungs nearly dying from the loss of air, she started to cough. Wiping her face, she swiveled to see where she was in the pool.

She cursed and slapped the top of the water. "Urg."

Lanelle had made it about to the three-quarters mark. That would be good, except she had been at three-quarters for the last week.

She did the front crawl back to the edge and lifted herself up, dangling her feet in the water.

Jalen Thomas flopped down beside her.

"You made it mad far without coming up," he grinned. "That's going to be our secret weapon in competition."

Lanelle looked at him and tried to smile.

Jalen grimaced. "Dang, that was a compliment."

A giggle escaped. She slapped her hand over her mouth.

"No, it's not that. I mean thanks," she mumbled.

"What's up? If you messed up, I didn't see it."

"I was trying to go the whole way. I've been stuck the past few days and not improving."

A whistle escaped his lips. "The whole way! Naw," he shook his head. "That's crazy, don't make unrealistic goals."

Lanelle's eyes narrowed. "Unrealistic?" she challenged as she raised her brow.

Jalen put his hands up in a surrender motion. "You can do anything you put your mind to."

Lanelle's shoulders relaxed and she smirked. "I'm just saying. I know I can do it, I'm just stuck. There has to be a way I can train or something to improve."

"So you really want to go the whole pool without breathing?" Jalen gazed at the water. "That's wild. You can do it though," he added quickly and peeked at her through the corner of his eye.

"Yo Lanelle!" Dion Sparks, Lanelle's twin brother, yelled from across the pool. "Dean Barkner wants you. Did you check your email?"

Lanelle rolled her eyes. "Why would I check my email when I am here?" she mumbled to Jalen.

Lanelle pulled herself to her feet and padded over to her towel that was hanging over a chair.

"How do you know he wants me?" she asked when Dion caught up to her.

"Because when you don't answer, everyone comes bothering me."

"So you be in my business all the time?" she hissed, raising an eyebrow.

Dion sucked his teeth and pushed her playfully.

Lanelle dramatically fell into the girl's locker room door.

* * *

Lanelle knocked on Dean Barkner's door. She hasn't spoken to him since the whole mess between her mother, Janelle Sparks, and Monica Michaelson, who used to teach at Deceptive High.

The door was cracked so she peeked her head in slightly, then heard him bellow, "Come in."

Lanelle pushed it open the remainder of the way. "Uh, Mr. Barkner, Dion said, I mean you wanted to see me?" She was unsure of whether she wanted to admit that she didn't see the emails.

"Ah yes, Ms. Sparks," Mr. Barkner said as he swiveled around in his huge office chair. "Sorry for the sense of urgency." He gestured for her to have a seat. "I hope all is well."

He said it like a question, but Lanelle was not going to tell him anything different, so she just smiled.

"I need a favor. I have two new students. Damien James and Ayana Brighten."

Lanelle's brow furrowed. "Okay," she said slowly. "What's the favor?"

"I need you to take Ayana as your roommate."

Lanelle's eyes popped open and her hands flew to the arms of the chair. "What!" she cried. "But I am in a single."

Mr. Barkner propped up on his elbows and touched his fingertips together. "I know. We think it would be most beneficial to Ms. Brighten if she has someone to show her the ropes."

"I can do that without sharing my room. It's unfair to have to give up my room." Lanelle sat back and crossed her arms over her chest. "Are you forcing me to do this?" she scowled.

Mr. Barkner leaned back in his seat, interlacing his hands in front of him. "I do not want to make you do anything," he started. "I would love it if you would take one for the team and help us out."

Lanelle scoffed "What team?"

Mr. Barkner sighed. "Will you agree to take her under your wing, help her out?"

"Without her living with me. I like my single and I am a second year now. I shouldn't have to share with anyone."

Mr. Barkner rubbed his temples before looking back up at Lanelle.

"Okay, I hear you. I will put her on your floor, in a separate room. She is moving in right now. Both her and Damien, please go introduce yourself."

Lanelle walked out of the office and ran right into Dion.

She screamed, then clapped her hand over her mouth. Her heart leaped from her chest as she tried to scatter backwards.

Dion began laughing.

After her soul returned to her body, she punched him on the shoulder. "You jerk. Why would you do that?" she whispered

They turned and walked down the hall. Dion not trying to hold in his snickering.

"Ain't my fault you so scared all the time."

Lanelle glared at him. She raised her hand, rotating her fingers until a golf ball-sized fireball materialized.

Dion flicked his wrist, and an icicle appeared. A door closed somewhere behind them, and they both balled their hands up into a fist, extinguishing their weapons.

"Ass," Lanelle muttered.

"So, what did he say?" Dion urged.

"Oh, yeah. He wanted me to give up my single and room with some girl."

"What did you tell him?" Dion asked.

Lanelle scowled. "What do you mean? I told him no. Why would I give up my single room?"

"How about you didn't earn it in the first place, Mom got it for you."

Lanelle rolled her eyes. "Well I am second year now, and the answer is still no."

Dion walked Lanelle to her room and then headed to his own, a floor above hers.

Music greeted him as he walked into his room. His roommate, Booker Benjamin, was playing around with his phone. Dion bobbed his head back and forth.

"Yo Booker, who this? It slap."

Booker lifted his head and grabbed his phone to turn down the music.

"Just something I have been working on. You think it's good?" He asked, his voice catching slightly.

Dion's eyes got wide. "You did this. Like produced it? Good, Booker this is beyond good."

Booker's mouth twitched. "Well, don't tell anyone yet. We still watching a movie tonight?"

"Oh yeah, I think so. Let me ask." Dion opened up the group chat message titled 'crew' on his phone.

Dion: Movies?

Quashawn: Yeah, Nelly's room, right?

Lanelle: Don't call me that! Yes, up here.

Lanelle: Oh, I invited Jalen. Hope that's okay.

Tariana: Yup, I'm down.

Dion winced and looked at Booker. "Don't worry about that yo. He is on the swim team with her."

Kasa: We are in too. Are we still invited?

Imani: Me too. Dion, I'm almost there; let me in.

Lanelle: Of course, yall can come Kasa.

Quashawn: 💋 Nelly. See yall tonight.

Booker threw his phone on the bed. "How have y'all been?" Dion asked.

Booker sighed heavily. "Great," he said, "just like friends."

"She will come around. She still likes you, though, I know that."

"Yeah, whatever." Booker groaned and sighed.

"On another note. This new student is coming, Damien. Dean wants me to basically be his friend."

Booker raised his eyebrow. "He's moving our room?"

Dion shook his head. "Naw, He will just be hanging around a lot. Lanelle has to do the same with this girl coming with him. Barkner tried to get her to take her as a roommate."

"And she said yes?"

Dion started laughing. "Hell naw."

Booker chuckled. "So what's the deal? He's coming to just the movie, or you got to do more?"

Dion shrugged. "I don't know. We will see how it goes."

Dion lounged on the bed with his phone, and Booker turned to his laptop. Booker glanced at the screen, which displayed his music playlist.

His finger hovered over the play, and he decided to pick up his phone. He wanted to text Lanelle. He knew she was still mad.

He sighed.

She said she wasn't mad, but their relationship was turned upside down. Booker's biological father was plotting to sabotage Lanelle, her brother, and her parents. He understood she felt betrayed, but once they got close, he should have told her.

He opened the messaging app and pulled her name up. He typed in a message three times and deleted it before throwing the phone back on the bed.

There was a knock at the door. "Come in," Dion yelled.

Imani, Dion's girlfriend, a junior, walked in.

"Hey, Booker," she said as she flips her shoes off.

Booker inclines his head. "What's up, Imani?"

"How was class?" Imani asked Dion as she flops on his bed.

"It was good," he replied.

Booker envied Dion and Imani. Imani had betrayed Dion, which was worse than what he had done to Lanelle, and they were good now.

Booker looked up and rolled his eyes at Dion and Imani. "Imma head to the library," he said as he stood and stuffed his computer in his book bag.

"Naw, Book. You don't have to leave."

"It's cool. I need to get some stuff done. I'll catch up with y'all tonight," he said, leaving the room.

Imani scrunched her eyebrows. "What was that about?"

Dion shrugged.

Imani picked at her nail. "Uh, Dion." she began.

"Yeah," he responded without looking up.

"I uh," she stumbled over her words. "I have a question."

Dion looked at her, raising one eyebrow. "Yeah, what's up?"

Imani just picked at her nail.

"Yo, Imani, what's up?" Dion repeated.

Imani took a deep breath. "We're okay, right? I mean. With

all the stuff that happened last year?"

"Yeah," Dion replied. He furrowed his brow. "Why?"

Imani shrugged. "I don't know. I just wanted to make sure."

Dion sat up on the bed. "Imani, quit playing."

"It's just that I overheard Joann saying that she was your partner in class, and you two hit it off." she said mockingly, mimicking Joann with a hair flip.

Dion's mouth turned down. "Joann is cool. We are pairs in combat. That's all."

"I know she's always saying something. I just wanted to make sure. I don't know." She sighed heavily and shrugged.

Dion's phone rang. He checked the screen, turned the phone over, and then looked back at Imani.

Imani glared at the phone. "Who is that?"

Dion rolled his eyes and laid back across the bed. "Imani, don't start. I'm sorry that Joann got in your head, but that has nothing to do with me. Don't turn this into a thing."

Dion put his headphones in and picked his phone up.

* * *

Lanelle flopped across her bed and sighed.

She wondered who these two kids were, Damien and Ayana. Barkner said they were coming in as second year just like her. She wondered what their deal was and why she had to take on the responsibility of showing her around.

Lanelle grabbed her phone and opened the InstaBook app. She typed Ayana's name into the search bar and scrolled through the options. Then, she hit the second one on the list and looked at the profile.

She didn't know what she was looking for. She didn't know what the girl looked like or any details to pinpoint her.

Might as well start getting ready for tonight, she thought. She needed to get the snacks and drinks together.

As she got up from her bed she thought it would be awkward with Booker and Jalen coming tonight.

Should she care what Booker thought, or Jalen, for that matter? Her and Booker were friends. They talked about that. She told him she needed time to think about what she wanted to do.

So, she shouldn't feel any type of way about inviting Jalen around.

Then why do you feel some type of way?

She did tell Dion about giving Imani another chance. Shouldn't she do the same to Booker?

She didn't say she wouldn't get back with Booker. She just needed time.

Time to do what?

Get to know Jalen?

Welcome Committee or Chaos Crew?

Ayana sat in her new room, staring aimlessly at her phone. Her roommate wasn't there, so she had time to get everything together.

The Dean told her a girl named Lanelle would be her "new buddy" for getting around the school. Lanelle invited her to a movie night she and her friends were having. Damien was coming too, she asked. She was not going by herself.

She did not need a babysitter. Being thrown into this new school, into someone else's friend group, was not something she was looking forward to. It felt like she was wearing someone else's skin.

She wondered how Damien was taking things.

She grabbed her phone, about to call him, when she realized she should head over to Lanelle's room for this movie.

Ayana groaned, slipped on her slides, and headed for the door.

She yelped and then touched her heart.

Damien stood at the door with raised, mid knock.

"You scared me! Were you waiting out here, you weirdo?" she exclaimed, stifling a grin.

Damien narrowed his eyes. "So what are you trying to say, imma creeper or something?"

"I mean," Ayana started.

"Oh hush," Damien cut her off.

Ayana grinned and leaned into him, her forehead pressing against his shoulder and frowned. "What's up?" he asked.

"I don't want to go," she whined.

"Why not? Is something wrong?"

Ayana buried her head further into his shoulder. "Why are we being forced to make friends?"

"It won't be that bad," Damien began. "You can't say you'd rather be with the people at our school," he smirked.

Ayana snorted. "Yeah, I'd rather be with Rachel."

Damien threw his head back with a laugh. "How do you know I wasn't talking about Tiffany?"

Ayana scrunched her brows. "I do miss Tiffany."

"These people cannot be that bad. I mean, hell, we are in a spy school."

Ayana grinned. "Yeah, who thought we would be in a spy school because of you."

Damien put his arm around her shoulder and the other against his chest in mock offense. "Because of me," he exclaimed as he led her out of the room.

"Yes, because of you. You and that Secret Garden."

"Don't hate on The Garden. It got us both here."

Outside Lanelle's door, Damien knocked. "It's just a movie. Quiet. in the dark - easy."

Lanelle answered, her two puffs bouncing. She smiled big. "Ayana and Damien, come in and meet the crew!" she said in one breath.

Ayana's smile tightened and she squeezed Damien's hand and walked into the room. Lanelle was already talking.

"...are here. This is my brother Dion and his girl Imani.

Then we have Quashawn and his sister Tariana. Kasa and her boyfriend Deslin. Booker and Jalen. Welcome to the crew!"

Ayana smiled awkwardly and waved. "I'm Ayana."

Damien nudged her. "And I'm the boyfriend, Damien."

"Oh yeah," Ayana giggled awkwardly. "Or you can be independent and introduce yourself."

Lanelle snorted. "Oh, I'm going to like you. Come sit down anywhere."

They watched as Lanelle sat between the girl introduced as Tariana and the guy introduced as Jalen.

Damien and Ayana sat on a bean bag on the side of the bed. Ayana plopped down on his lap.

"So," Dion started. "What's the deal with you two? How did you end up here?"

Ayana looked back at Damien. "My mother just told us one day," he said.

"Were they spies?" Lanelle asked.

They both shrugged.

"Something has to be up," Lanelle continued. "Everyone here has a parent in the student agency or whatever. That's how we all go here."

"Your parents are spies?" Ayana asked.

Everyone around the room nodded.

"And the twin's parents are legends. They are legacies." Imani said, gazing at Dion, who quickly smiled and turned his head.

Ayana and Damien looked at each other. Damien raised one brow,, but Ayana wasn't sure whether he meant that interaction or the fact that everyone's parents were spies.

The group debated movies. Dion insisted on The Ghouls.

"Horror? Only you two freaks like this," Tariana groaned.

Damian leaned forward."I've wanted to see this."

Lanelle side-eyed him. "Of course you would.".

"That's a nice piece," Jalen said, nodding at Damien's bracelet.

"Thanks," he said flatly. "It was my grandfather's."

Ayana looked straight at the TV. Damien squeezed her side, urging her to relax.

The light turned off, and the movie began. "It's okay," he mouthed. "Relax."

* * *

After the movie, everyone sat in Lanelle's room.

"I can't believe you want to make it the whole pool," Jalen said.

"You swim?" Damien asked, leaning back to see Lanelle and Jalen.

"We both do," she replied. "We are on the swim team here. Do you swim?"

"Naw," he replied. "Ana does; basketball is more of my thing. They got sports here, right?"

"Not really," Jalen said. "With all the combat and things, it's more clubs. Swimming is a team, and we have a basketball team, but that's it. Lanelle, here is the star, though. She's practicing to make it to the entire pool in one breath," Jalen beamed.

Booker stood and walked to the front door. "I've got to go, y'all. Early class."

"What clubs?" Ayana asked.

Lanelle stared after Booker, debating on whether she should go after him.

"We have culture-type clubs," Kasa said. "We're in one for natives," she said, pointing to Deslin.

"There is dance, theater too. Also, things like chess," she scrunched her nose. "I am sure there is a club that interests you."

"Book club?" Ayana asked.

"Yes," Lanelle squealed. "I am in that! I can give you the details if you want. Now," she said, looking over the room. "Y'all ain't got to go home, but y'all got to get out of here. I also have an early class tomorrow. Ayana, do you know where your first class is?"

"I don't even know how to read that paper. All I know is that it's at 9 a.m."

Lanelle chuckled. "Let's meet here at 8 for breakfast, and I'll explain everything and walk you to class."

"You got a morning class, Damien? We can all get together," Dion chimed in.

"Okay, that will work," Damien responded.

"This was fun," Jalen says to Lanelle. "Thanks for inviting me around."

Lanelle rolled her eyes. "Of course, you liked that awful movie," she grumbled.

Jalen threw his head back and laughed. "It was good. All y'all were safe, right?" he asked, gesturing to her and approaching Tariana.

Tariana crossed her arms over her chest. "No, not okay, not safe, terrible pick."

"It was not that bad," Quashawn called from the room. "Yo T, you coming? I'll walk you to your room."

"Yea, give me a sec," she called back.

Jalen smiled, touched Lanelle's shoulder, and left. Tariana glared at Lanelle, who watched Jalen leave with Kasa & Deslin all starry-eyed. She jabbed her with her elbow.

"Later," Tariana cornered Lanelle. "Eyes off Jalen, focus on Booker."

Lanelle sighed. "It's...complicated."

"Complicated?" Tariana mocked. "You're at spy school. Everything's complicated."

"T, dang!" Quashawn huffed impatiently by the door. "Tell Nelly bye, and let's go."

Lanelle signed, looking up at the ceiling. Tariana grinned. "He's not giving it up; get used to it."

Tariana patted Lanelle on the shoulder and walked away.

Ctrl + Alt + Where's My Brain?

Ayana and Damien shared a quick breakfast before diving into their jam-packed schedules. Neither had core classes that's why they could jump into second year, just combat and covert training.

During computer class, Ayana stared at her screen, fingers frozen over the keyboard. The assignment: research "Michael St. Jonston" using a photo and basic details. Simple, right? But the search results were a chaotic flood of information—dozens of Michaels, none matching the cold, calculating eyes in the photo.

She clenched her fists under the desk, letting out a frustrated sigh. Around her, classmates were typing furiously, flipping through notes and tablets like professionals. Everyone seemed to know exactly what they were doing—except her.

"Everything alright?" A smooth, feminine voice broke her concentration. Ayana jumped and turned to see the teacher standing beside her.

"Sorry, didn't mean to scare you, Hun," the teacher said, her warm gaze drifting to Ayana's blank screen. Her brow furrowed slightly. "Need help?"

Ayana hesitated, then squeezed her eyes shut. Taking a deep breath, she finally blurted out, "I need more direction." The words tumbled out quickly.

The teacher's eyes crinkled with a kind smile. "This is an open-ended assignment. In the field, you'll often have to dig up information without clear instructions. Your goal here is to sift through everything you find, decide what's relevant, and organize it logically."

Ayana frowned, her gaze falling back on the screen. "So...like, I'm supposed to write a biography on this guy?"

"Exactly! Start there," the teacher encouraged, clasping her hands together. "But keep it concise—just the important points. No need to get fancy with it."

Nodding slowly, Ayana bit her lip. "Okay." She grabbed the mouse and clicked back to her search results. The teacher squeezed her shoulder as she walked away.

Alright, a biography. I can do that.

Ayana scanned the first link on the search page. *Wikinternet Search.* She rolled her eyes. That site was a joke—absolutely useless. Skipping to the next result, she landed on a page that listed multiple Michael St. Jonstons, all with blurred-out details and a paywall.

She groaned. "I'm not paying for this," she muttered. Besides, how could she tell which one was the right Michael?

Her eyes drifted to the photo on the information sheet the teacher had handed out. Thin, square glasses. Short, gelled hair slicked back. He looked like someone's accountant or a college professor. Ayana returned to her search bar and typed in keywords related to social media.

Minutes passed. She clicked through dozens of profiles and articles, each leading her further into a web of dead ends. But finally, after what felt like an eternity, she found him. The picture on his profile was younger than the one she had, but everything else—birthplace, age, and college—matched perfectly.

By the end of class, Ayana had filled three pages in her notebook. Michael St. Jonston was a piece of work. As a child, he'd been kidnapped from a park by an elderly woman. He was found a week later thanks to a vigilant cashier who recognized him from the news.

In junior high, he trapped a girl inside the school library, barricading the door. She'd screamed for help, and it took staff several minutes to reach her.

Then came the most disturbing incident—his arrest for kidnapping. Ayana became engrossed in piecing together every article she could find. The details were annoyingly vague like someone had cut out all the important parts and left her with scraps. The same vague story kept popping up: a girl had escaped and ran to a nearby house. The homeowner called the police, and St. Jonston was captured shortly afterward. But the deeper details were locked behind a paywall.

She grunted. *Why is everything behind a damn paywall?*

Ayana glanced at the clock and sighed. Time was running out, and she needed more information. Still, at least she wasn't stuck anymore.

Ayana clicked on the page where the assignment was posted and opened the template the teacher had provided. It was simple and straightforward: sections for key facts, dates, connections, and a summary. Just what she needed to gather her chicken scratches in her notebook together.

"Don't forget—this is due at 11:59 p.m. tonight!" the teacher called out, her voice echoing over the sound of chairs scraping and computers shutting down.

Ayana quickly saved her work to the Cloud. She shut down

her computer and packed up her notebook, relieved to have made some progress. Lanelle's mini-tour had helped a little, but Ayana still felt like the school was a confusing giant maze. Hallways stretched in every direction, and everything kind of looked the same. Slinging her bag over her shoulder, she rushed out of the classroom, glancing nervously at her watch.

She stopped by the equipment station and carefully dropped off the borrowed computer. For a moment, she hesitated, double-checking that it was turned off.

Exhaling, she adjusted her bag and headed into the hallway. The crowd of students moving between classes surged around her like a fast-moving river, and she tried her best to stay afloat in the current. Getting lost on this massive campus wasn't part of today's plan—and being late to her next class on top of that?

Ayana sat through three more classes before she had a break. Her schedule had all the regular classes in the morning and her fighting classes in the afternoon. She had two hours before it was time to head over to the building where the fighting, or combat like everyone here called it, happened.

In front of the imposing building, a small seating area was nestled within a ring of ancient stone benches, worn smooth by time and generations of students. The benches curved gently around a circular stone fountain, in the middle, a carved griffin with weathered wings outstretched, sat, frozen mid-leap. Water trickled softly from its mouth, the sound delicate and calming among the quiet rustle of the surrounding ivy-covered walls.

Tall, wrought-iron lampposts framed the area, their glass lanterns flickering with light.

A few tables with mismatched wrought-iron chairs were scattered around, each tucked into little nooks. Ayana sat on one and pulled out her phone.

Her day had been so chaotic that she hadn't even glanced at her phone, let alone replied to anyone. Now that she finally had a moment to breathe, Ayana scrolled through her messages. First, she sent quick replies to her mom and sister, Ryan, who had checked in on her. Ryan teased her about drowning in homework, while her mom sent a mini-lecture about time management, complete with advice she didn't ask for but would probably appreciate later.

Lanelle's message was about the book club, saying they could meet at the pool and walk over together if Ayana was interested. Another buzz came in from Tariana, inviting her to join the dance team that evening. Ayana replied "yes" to both, a grin tugging at the corner of her mouth. Her mom's warning about time management echoed faintly in the back of her mind, but she brushed it aside. What was the point if she didn't make friends and have fun?

Then she saw Damien's message. Her smile faded as she opened the thread. His words were short and urgent. ***I need to see you. Something's wrong***.

Her brow furrowed. The message had been sent an hour ago. Ayana cursed under her breath and checked the time again. She couldn't waste another second. Grabbing her bag, she took off, her heartbeat racing as fast as her thoughts. Whatever was going on, it sounded serious. She needed to find Damien—now.

* * *

Damien paced back and forth in his room, his grandfather's bracelet humming against his wrist when there was a bang at the door.

22

"Damien," he heard Ayana say and he rushed to open it.

She brushed right past him talking a mile a minute. "What's wrong? I was in class, I didn't have time to check my phone. What happened? Are you okay?"

He put his hands on her shoulder. "Ana, slow down. We need to go to The Garden. Something is wrong."

Ayana screwed up her face, opening and closing her mouth a few times. She took a step back, letting Damien's hands fall. "What? How?" She stumbled over her words, confused.

"The bracelet is vibrating," he explained. "That means Michael is calling and something is wrong. I need to go."

"Not without me," she exclaimed.

Damien rolled his eyes. "I know, that's why I wanted you to come. I got...we got to go now."

"How do *we*," she stretched out that last word. "Even get there? I thought we needed your closet."

He shook his head. "We need A closet. This one will work."

Damien rotated his watch, pressed a button, then reached for Ayana's hand. "Let's go," he said without waiting for a response.

He opened the door and Ayana closed her eyes. It had been a while since she had traveled to The Garden, but her stomach always felt uneasy. She took a deep breath and counted to three. When she opened her eyes, they stood in The Garden.

They stepped out of the portal, Ayana's breath caught as the world she hadn't seen in so long unfolded before her. It was the same magical landscape that had once felt like a second home, yet now it appeared sharper, more alive, almost as if it had changed in her absence—or perhaps she had.

The towering purple trees stood like ancient sentinels, their bark shimmering faintly in the moonlight, just as she remembered. The trees seemed more imposing, their intricate carvings and twisting branches more pronounced. There was a quiet hum of magic in the air, a familiar energy that buzzed faintly under her skin.

The pink moon hung low in the sky, massive and luminous. Its craters, dark and deep, still created the illusion of shifting depths. That moonlight had always been enough to light the path, but it seemed brighter now, casting everything in a glittering, dreamlike glow.

Her boots hit the blue stones—familiar, but threaded with cracks like veins. They seemed cooler to the touch, as if carrying the memories of every step she had ever taken. On either side of the path, the vibrant green grass shimmered softly in the moonlight. She crouched and let her fingers graze the surface. The grass was still soft, like clouds, but with an inexplicable warmth.

Ayana rose and walked forward slowly, savoring how the ground beneath her feet cushioned each step as if it wanted to carry her weight. She knew the feeling well, yet it still filled her with the same awe as it had the first time.

Ahead, the purple trees clustered in dense formations, their branches arching together like a protective canopy. Their shifting leaves glinted in the light, whispering softly in the breeze. She moved toward them cautiously, nostalgia mingling with curiosity. These trees had always held secrets, and she had often wondered how much they had seen in the centuries they stood here.

As she reached up toward the glimmering leaves, the deep, familiar rumble echoed through the grove. The sound vibrated through her chest like distant thunder. Her pulse quickened. It was the same sound that had startled her so long ago, and even now it sent a shiver of fear and wonder through her. The trees groaned as they began to shift, parting slowly and deliberately, as if recognizing her return.

Damien let her take the lead, smiling at the glimmer in her wide eyes as she walked through The Garden.

When the trees moved aside, the hidden landscape beyond unfurled. Tall grasses swayed in the gentle wind, stretching far into the horizon. The colors shifted with each movement—emerald green, glowing gold, deep crimson—just as they had before. Under the pink moon's light, the entire scene sparkled like a dream. Ayana exhaled slowly, watching the dance of the grass. She had forgotten just how breathtaking this place could be.

The grass parted to form a path, welcoming her back into the heart of the world. Behind her, the tall blades rose once more, sealing off the way they had come. The sensation of being protected and trapped washed over her.

A soft, distant chirp broke the stillness, pulling her attention. Ayana's gaze shifted across the undulating field. From within the tall grass, something small emerged—a squat, gray figure with short, stocky limbs and skin that gleamed like polished stone. Its large amber eyes blinked, studying her. It was unchanged, just as she remembered it, as if no time had passed since her last visit. It was Micheal.

This world had been waiting for her, but it had grown just like she had. It welcomed her back in its strange, subtle way, every sound and movement whispering the same message: she belonged here—but she would have to earn that place again.

Michael?

yana's gaze lingered on the shimmering landscape, lost in the nostalgia of a place that had once felt eternal. But as she went deeper into the field, something tugged at the edge of her senses—a subtle wrongness that slowly crept in.

Far off, over the hills the tall, swaying grasses that once shifted effortlessly from green to gold to crimson, began to falter. Some blades turned a dull, lifeless brown, curling at the edges like parchment scorched by invisible fire. The glow that had once made the entire world sparkle dimmed, and patches of glittering light scattered unevenly, as if struggling to hold on.

Ayana paused, her eyes squinting as she took in the change. The gentle breeze that had carried the sweet, earthy scent now smelled faintly of decay.

The purple trees that had stood tall and luminous now looked darker, their leaves sagging as if drained of life. The once-glittering bark dulled to a muddy gray-purple, and faint cracks began to spread across their trunks. The deep rumble echoed again, but this time it was weaker, more like a distant groan of pain.

Ayana took a slow step forward, unease settling heavily in

her chest. The sky above remained dark, but the pink moon's vibrant glow dimmed, its edges blurring. Shadows stretched unnaturally long across the stone path, twisting and shifting as if alive.

Michael now hesitated, his large amber eyes darting nervously around. He shifted his weight, making an anxious low snuffling noise. Suddenly, he retreated back into the tall grass, vanishing as quickly as it had appeared.

Ayana's pulse quickened and she looked at Damien. He too was peering off into the distance at the changing, and perhaps, dying state of The Garden.

"Micheel," Damien called out. "Come back, what is happening."

Michael crept back through the tall grass, his stocky limbs moving with surprising grace. His gray, stone-like skin gleamed faintly under the dim pink moon, textured like ancient rock polished by centuries of magic. His large, warm amber eyes blinked slowly.

His gaze swept across the landscape, narrowing as he took in the withering grasses and crumbling trees. There was tension in his usual calm demeanor, his thick, stone-like brows furrowing deeply.

His footsteps crunched under the grass as he approached front of Ayana and Damien, his amber eyes fixed on hers with a gravity that sent a shiver down her spine.

Michael, in this form, was both protector and warning—an embodiment of the ancient magic that had kept this world alive. But now, that magic was slipping away, and the concern in his gaze spoke volumes: time was running out.

Ayana knelt down in front of Michael and peered at him with concern. "Michael, what's happening?"

"The Garden is beginning to perish," Michael said, his voice carrying the weight of a centuries-old warning.

Damien shook his head. "What does that mean?"

Ayana glanced between them, her stomach twisting in fear. "It's…dying?" she asked, a tremble in her voice.

"No. Impossible," Damien snapped sharply. Michael stared up at him with steady, unblinking amber eyes.

"It's not impossible," Michael replied, his voice low and grave. "This isn't natural decay. Someone has come here—an intruder—and they've poisoned the magic that sustains this world. The Garden is connected to every vein of magic within this realm. Poison the core, and everything begins to rot from within."

Damien's fists clenched, his jaw tightening. "Who would do that? And why?"

Michael's gaze darkened, flickering like dying embers. "I don't know their identity. But I do know this: they didn't come here by accident," he rasped, claws digging into the earth as if anchoring himself to a crumbling world.

Ayana turned in a slow circle, her eyes tracing the death creeping through the once-vibrant landscape. The grasses dulled and crumbled before her eyes, their golden hues fading to ashen gray. The trees groaned again, their bark splitting and flaking off like brittle shards of glass. The air, once filled with the faint hum of life and magic, now smelled of rot and decay.

"What kind of poison could destroy something so powerful?" she asked, dread curling in her gut.

"It's not like any physical poison," Michael explained. "This is a corruption of magic itself—dark, insidious. The longer it lingers, the harder it will be to purge. Time is already slipping away."

Ayana swallowed hard. The world she had always known to be alive and powerful was crumbling right in front of her. "How do we stop it?"

Michael's gaze softened slightly. "We have to reach the heart of The Garden. The core source of magic is there. If we can cleanse and restore it, we might be able to reverse the damage. But the corruption won't make it easy for us. It will fight. Harder than anything you've faced before."

Damien cursed and paced a few steps away before turning back, determination hardening his features. "Then that's what we will do."

Ayana nodded, though her fear hadn't lessened. She met Damien's gaze, both of t silently vowing not to back down. This world had become a part of them, and they weren't going to let it die without a fight.

"I cannot accompany you but I do have things for you to prepare for your journey." He gestured for them to wait as he walked through the grass. "This journey will be long," he said. "Because you aren't permanent residence here, it will likely take multiple trips."

"Wait," Ayana butted in. "Every time we come back we must, what? Start over again. Every time we come here, we enter at the same spot."

Michael shook his head. "It's because it's the only spot he knows." He says looking back at Damien. "Think of where you want to enter, and you will enter there."

Ayana looked back at Damien who scowled at the decaying land.

As they walked together, the tall grasses receded completely, replaced by a patch of low, silvery-blue plants that shimmered faintly under the waning moonlight. Ahead, nestled within a cluster of ancient trees, stood Michael's house—a structure that looked as though it had been grown rather than built.

The house rose from the ground like a living part of the landscape. The walls were formed from smooth, stone-like bark, twisted and intertwined with deep roots that coiled around the base like protective armor. Large, arched windows glowed softly with a warm amber light, casting faint patterns of leaves onto the ground. Ivy with faintly glowing veins climbed the walls in elegant spirals, blending seamlessly with the structure's natural curves.

A wide, curved, dark wooden door, shimmering like polished obsidian, stood at the entrance. Intricate symbols, imbued with ancient magic adorned its surface. Above the door, a small circular window framed the pink moon perfectly, almost like a protective eye.

"Come," Michael said as he stepped inside the threshold.

Ayana grabbed Damien's hand and squeezed. When he looked at her, the smile did not reach his eyes.

Inside, the main room was circular, its high ceiling lined with wooden beams that resembled the ribcage. Shelves carved directly into the walls held an array of strange artifacts: glowing crystals, weathered books, and jars filled with substances that shimmered and swirled. A large hearth dominated one side of the room, though no fire burned in it. Instead, a cluster of floating balls emitted a soft, golden light, gently warming the space.

In the center of the room, a low polished stone table sat atop a woven rug that shifted colors—sometimes deep blue, sometimes rich green—depending on the angle. Cushioned seats were arranged in a way that suggested both comfort and deep conversation.

Plants grew in every corner, their leaves luminous in the dim light. Some swayed gently as though stirred by an unseen breeze, while others emitted a faint, soothing hum that vibrated Ayana's skin. She looked to see if Damien felt the same. His eyes were trained on Michael.

The air smelled clean and fresh but carried a faint trace of earth and something metallic.

Michael motioned for them to sit near the table as he moved toward a side alcove, holding an assortment of neatly arranged ingredients and tools. Ayana felt as if the house seemed to breathe with life, ancient and powerful, yet welcoming.

Damien stood nearby, eyeing the strange artifacts with curious suspicion. Ayana could tell he wasn't quite at ease, but she also sensed he knew this place offered some measure of protection from the chaos outside.

This house was a sanctuary, one rooted in the deep magic of The Garden. Yet, Ayana couldn't shake the feeling that the decay outside was creeping closer.

Michael dropped a box on the table. The tape that held it together was frayed and peeling like a long-forgotten relic of rushed repairs.

"This box has everything you need it in. You must look through and read the material before you begin the journey to the core."

Damien grunted. "Michael we do not have all this time. Did you see outside, we need to go!" he yelled.

"You need to be safe. and to do that, you need this," Micheal pushed the box towards the pair.

Ayana picked up the box. "Thanks Michael, we will get on it." She turned and looked at Damien. "Right Damien, so we can help?"

Damien and sighed "Give it to me," he said.

The Bond in the Blaze - Forged in Frost and Flame

Dion and Lanelle were deep in the woods behind the school, near the sprawling fields. The dense canopy of trees muted the late afternoon light, casting long shadows across the forest floor. Fallen leaves crunched softly beneath their feet.

"Watch out!" Lanelle yelped, stepping back abruptly as a shard of ice whizzed past her. She shot a glare at her brother. "You trying to freeze me to death? I thought you said you had excellent control."

Dion winced, flexed his fingers, and tried again. Focusing, he tried to summon the cold without it spiraling out of control. A cluster of jagged icicles shot from his hand, embedding themselves into the ground with a dull thud. Long, sharp, and completely unintended.

"Uh, yeah...guess that's not what I was going for," Dion muttered under his breath.

"Mm-hmm. So I guess that 'excellent control' was a lie," Lanelle said, crossing her arms.

"Shh, just let me concentrate," he snapped, narrowing his eyes at the frost creeping up the bark of a nearby tree.

Lanelle sighed dramatically, rolling her eyes. "Let me catch something on fire, and then you freeze it. Let's see if that helps you summon the cold without ice."

Dion frowned but didn't argue. Lanelle, never one to wait for permission, scanned the forest floor for something to ignite. Her gaze landed on a partially buried rock tangled in the roots of a gnarled tree. She knelt beside it and grabbed the rock, tugging hard.

The rock didn't budge.

"Come on, stupid thing," Lanelle grumbled under her breath. Bracing one foot against the root for leverage, she pulled – hard. The rock popped free with a sudden jolt, sending her sprawling backward onto the ground.

"Ahh!" she screeched, landing with an awkward thud. "Oof."

Dion's head snapped around. He raised an eyebrow, clearly unimpressed. "What are you doing?"

Lanelle sat up, brushing dirt and dead leaves off her pants. "Getting you something to freeze, obviously."

Dion smirked. "Yeah, looks like you're the one who needs more control."

"Ha–ha," Lanelle deadpanned, standing and shaking off the last bits of forest debris. She held up the rock triumphantly. "Got it. Now, are you going to stop being useless and actually freeze something?"

Lanelle looked at the rock and it ignited in flames. She held it in her hand, carefully controlling it to not let the fire expand or land on anything else. She peeked up over her engulfed rock at her brother with a raised brow.

"Fine," Dion muttered, stepping closer. He lifted his hands, palms outward, and focused on the rock. A cool mist began to swirl around his fingers, condensing into frost that crawled toward the stone. He focused harder, trying to maintain the cold without accidentally launching another ice spike.

Lanelle's eyes sparkled mischievously. "Alright, showtime. Freeze it before it melts."

The flame danced, casting flickering shadows across the ice creeping over the rock's surface. Dion's brow furrowed as he pushed the cold further. Frost began to cover the entire stone, but the flame stubbornly refused to die out.

"Come on, Dion. You can't let me win this," Lanelle teased, the fire in her hands growing brighter.

"You think this is a competition?" Dion grunted. He clenched his jaw and pushed more energy into the cold, watching as the frost thickened. The air between them grew tense, charged with opposing forces of heat and cold.

The flame flickered once...twice...and then extinguished with a sharp hiss.

Lanelle blinked, then frowned down at the frozen rock. "Okay. Not bad," she admitted reluctantly. "You might not totally suck after all."

Dion exhaled, lowering his hands as steam rose from the rapidly melting frost. "Told you I could do it."

Lanelle shoved him playfully. "Don't get cocky. You barely pulled that off."

"Whatever," Dion said.

They laughed, the tension easing between them. Around them, the forest remained still and quiet, as if holding its breath after the clash of elements. The siblings stood side by side for a moment, basking in the cool, peaceful air.

"Okay," Lanelle finally said, nudging him with her elbow. "What's next, Ice King?"

Dion grinned. "I dunno. Maybe I should teach you how not to trip over tree roots."

"Or maybe I should teach you how to aim so you don't kill your own sister," Lanelle shot back with a smirk.

"We can practice some combat," Dion suggested.

Lanelle narrowed her eyes. "We are supposed to be practicing our magic. Practice fighting in the gym."

"Scared?" Dion teased and lunged for her.

Lanelle squealed and launched her protective barrier, a translucent dome shimmering like glass dipped in molten gold. The barrier's surface shifted and rippled, catching the faintest light in dazzling, iridescent patterns. It was nearly see-through, allowing her a full view of the forest. Inside, the air warmed just enough to feel comforting but not stifling, cocooning her in a magical shield.

Lanelle crossed her arms and glared at Dion. "Do Not Start," she warned.

Dion threw an ice ball at the dome. It bounced off, not even making a ripple. "The barrier is cheating Nelly," he said, drawing out the hated nickname.

To fight back, Lanelle would have to lower her shield, and Dion knew it. He smirked, his eyes glinting with mischief as he advanced. Suddenly, he leapt into the air, spinning gracefully mid-flight. His hand sliced downward like a blade, frost trailing his fingertips. He didn't expect much—just to rattle her barrier.

With a sharp crack, the shimmering dome fractured beneath his strike. The protective barrier shattered cleanly, segments falling apart in perfect, triangular slices, like a pizza divided by invisible lines. Each piece hovered momentarily, gleaming in the sunlight, before dissolving into a flurry of golden sparks that rained softly around them.

They froze in shock. Lanelle blinked rapidly, her mouth

slightly open.

"Did you just...cut through my barrier?" she finally asked, incredulous.

"I—I guess I did," Dion stammered, as he stared at where the barrier had been.

Lanelle shook her head, her voice rising. "Are you serious right now? I didn't even know that was possible."

Dion grinned smugly, regaining his confidence. "Hey, I don't know. Maybe I'm just that good," he teased, flexing his fingers.

Lanelle rolled her eyes but couldn't hide her amusement. "We need to call Mom and Dad, ASAP. We got to figure out how you just did that."

Dion put his hand on her shoulder. "Yeah, yeah, okay," he said he hit the ground with a thud.

Lanelle narrowed her eyes and took a defensive stance, one leg back, her hands raised and glowing with a flickering red-orange hue. "Never let your guard down, brother."

Dion chuckled as he got up. A thin layer of frost spread along his forearms as he clenched his fists. "Oh so we're doing this?" he asked.

They circled each other slowly, tension crackling in the air. Lanelle dashed forward, swinging a fiery punch toward Dion's torso. He ducked, the heat grazing his skin, and countered with a sweep kick. Lanelle jumped over it with ease, twisting mid-air and launching a stream of fire from her hands.

Dion thrust his palms out, a gust of freezing wind surging from his fingertips. The fire and ice collided, steam hissing and swirling around them like an angry fog.

"See, why couldn't you do that two minutes ago," she taunted, stepping through the mist with a roundhouse kick aimed at his head.

Dion barely managed to block it, staggering back from the impact. Retaliating, he clapped his hands together, sending a shockwave of ice spikes toward her feet. Lanelle's eyes widened as she narrowly dodged, flipping to the side, and hurling a fireball in his direction.

The fireball exploded on contact, forcing Dion to raise an ice wall just in time to block the brunt of it. The wall cracked under the pressure but didn't break. "Getting serious now, huh?" he called out from behind his shield.

"Of course!" Lanelle grinned, flames licking around her fists. She ran forward and leapt, her fist blazing as she came down hard with a flaming punch. Dion dropped his shield and rolled out of the way, the ground where he had stood erupting in fire.

He came up behind her, the ice quickly forming on his hands. Moving quickly, he grabbed her arm, frost spreading rapidly across her sleeve. Lanelle hissed and spun around, using her other hand to release a concentrated blast of heat. The ice shattered, freeing her arm as Dion stumbled back from the sudden burst of warmth.

"Let's turn up the heat," she challenged, her hands igniting like twin torches.

"Not if I cool you down first," Dion shot back, stomping the ground. Ice rippled outward in a circle, the grass beneath them freezing instantly. Lanelle skidded as she lost traction, her sneakers slipping on the slick surface.

She crouched low, focusing her energy into a fiery burst around her body, melting the ice underfoot. Steam rose in violent clouds as fire and ice clashed all around them.

"Time to finish this," Lanelle growled. She sprinted toward Dion, feinting left before swinging a fire-coated uppercut. Dion anticipated her move, stepping aside and catching her wrist mid-swing. Twisting her arm gently, he flipped her off-balance. She landed on her back but quickly tucked and rolled to avoid the ice spikes he conjured.

Breathing heavily, Lanelle and Dion stood across from each other again, the clearing around them scorched and frozen in chaotic patches. They grinned, eyes alight with excitement.

"Not bad," Dion admitted, wiping sweat—or was it melted ice—from his brow.

"You're not too shabby yourself, icicle boy," Lanelle teased, brushing soot from her clothes. "But next time, I'm bringing the full blaze."

"I'll hold you to that," Dion said with a smirk. They relaxed as the adrenaline wore off.

"Same time next week?" Lanelle asked, raising an eyebrow.

"You bet. Gotta keep you on your toes," Dion replied with a playful wink.

The siblings laughed as they walked off, leaving the battle-field of fire and ice behind.

In Sync

Lanelle burst through the water's surface, gasping for air as droplets streamed down her face. She blinked rapidly, pushing her wet hair out of her eyes, and glanced around. She had come in third place. Again.

Frustration gnawed at her as she treaded water. This was why she had to work on her breath control. No matter how much she improved, Stephanie and Taylor were still faster, cutting through the water like they were born in it. Lanelle clenched her jaw, watching them casually swim toward the pool's edge, their victory effortless.

"Good job ladies," the coach's voice echoed. "Hit the showers I will see you tomorrow."

She pulled herself out of the water. "You were so good," Taylor said.

The pair were waiting for her. "The three of us will take all the metals at the next competition. You were right behind us," Stephanie said excitedly. The girls were in their fourth year at Douglas, with only two more until the Decision Ceremony—the moment that would define their futures. They'd have to choose between joining the family business or stepping into the real world.

Lanelle plastered a smile on her face. "Thanks," she said as she walked off.

Did they really just congratulate her on losing? This is why she had to work on her breathing. She could get fast enough to beat them.

When she came out of the locker room she saw Ayana walking, staring at the pool.

"Oh, hey girl," she said waving her hand to get her attention. "I hope I didn't have you waiting long."

Ayana chuckled. "You mean assuming I knew exactly where this place was and got here on time?"

Lanelle clapped her hand over her mouth, trying to muffle her laugh. "You'll get used to it. I swear."

They headed out of the pool area and headed towards the library, where the book club was meeting.

"So we just finished a book. Today is our discussion and we get our next book," Lanelle pulled out her phone. "Here is the app we use," she had a QR code pulled out. When Ayana scanned it it brought her to a Booked & Scheduled app. She clicked to download.

"What book y'all just finished?" Ayana asked.

Lanelle's eyes widened, sparkling with excitement as a grin spread across her face. "Girl, it's called King Author and his Slave."

Ayana wrinkled her nose.

"No," Lanelle started. "Don't judge it by the title."

"Monica's this smart, ambitious girl who's grieving after losing her mom in a tragic accident. She ends up in this early college program. But from the start, something ain't right," Lanelle makes a face and looks at Ayana before continuing.

"Like, she starts seeing these weird supernatural stuff. Then, on her first night, she witnesses this magical creature attack someone—and this secret society of students shows up and it goes down. Turns out they're part of this ancient order, descended from King Arthur's knights. And yeah, they fight demons and protect the human world."

Lanelle takes a breath and peeks at Ayana.

"Okay, I'm hooked. Keep going," Ayana said.

Lanelle smiles. "But here's where it gets *wild*. Monica discovers that magic might have been involved in her mom's death and that the order might hold the answers she's been searching for. So she sneaks into the society to get to the truth. Along the way, she discovers all this hidden history about her own ancestry, including some seriously powerful and ancient magic connected to her lineage. Of course, there's boy drama. There's Mick, this fine knight-in-training who becomes her ally and Jacob.

But what I *love* about the book is how it tackles race, identity, and grief. Monica's a Black girl stepping into a world steeped in old, white-dominated traditions, and she calls out the racism and elitism head-on. It's so powerful and real. Plus, the twists will have you screaming by the end."

"Dang, I wish I was there for that book," Ayana said.

"I have it in my room. You can borrow it."

The girls stepped into the library, their footsteps muffled by the thick carpet. Shelves towered around them like quiet sentinels, the scent of old books and polished wood in the air. They made their way to a smaller room off to the side where the book club was gathering. The warm, golden light from the hanging lamps cast a cozy glow over the circular table surrounded by cushioned chairs.

"Hey y'all," Lanelle said cheerfully as they entered. "This is Ayana."

Heads turned toward them, and a few people smiled and waved. The club admin, a math teacher, stood at the front with an easygoing air of authority.

"Alright, everyone," the teacher began, clapping her hands lightly for attention. "Let's hear some initial thoughts about the book—no spoilers."

The room came alive with conversation as students eagerly voiced their opinions. Ayana quickly found herself drawn in. Even though she hadn't read the book, she listened closely, picking up key themes and ideas from what others were saying. Before long, she chimed in, offering observations and questions that made everyone pause and rethink their points. Her outsider's perspective challenged some of the assumptions being made, sparking deeper discussions.

To her surprise, she was holding her own in the conversation. Lanelle beamed at her from across the table, clearly pleased that Ayana was fitting in so naturally.

"Our next book is *Serial Killer, Con Artist and Jelena by Ashley Johnson*," the teacher announced after the conversation wound down. There was a brief shuffle as students pulled out their phones, immediately searching for where to order it.

"You can get it off One Stop and have it mailed to the school," Lanelle whispered to Ayana.

Ayana nodded and shot off a quick text to her mom, asking if she could order the book for her. As she glanced around the room, she noticed how effortlessly everyone seemed to be handling the task—no hesitation, no worry.

"Everyone just has money to order stuff?" Ayana muttered, her brow furrowing.

"I have an on-campus job," Lanelle replied casually. "Some people just ask their parents or get an allowance."

Ayana's ears perked up. "We can get jobs on campus?" she asked.

Lanelle smiled and nodded. "Yeah, of course. There are different kinds—library assistant, tutoring, and even helping in admin offices. I'll show you where to look on the school system when we leave."

After applying for a few jobs, the girls walked back towards Howard.

"All my stuff is electronic on my tablet," Lanelle was explaining her color-coded class system. "I just borrow a computer if I need it in class. Back home I used to do the same thing but with notebooks. Now all I carry is this," she said holding her tablet up.

Ayana thought. She liked how simple it seemed but she loved her notebook. Would her mom buy her one if she asked or should she just wait until she got a job?

"What you got goin' on later?" Lanelle asked.

"I'm going to grab something quick to eat because I told Tariana I would go check out the dance team with her. What about you? Are you on the dance team too?"

Lanelle sucked her teeth. "Girl, I have two left feet." She put her finger to her mouth. "Shh don't tell nobody though." They started cackling.

"Me and Tariana always meet up at 7 and have a two-hour "get our shit done" time during the week. It's a study session basically."

"Can I join," Ayana asked. "It makes no sense how much homework I have. Do y'all have it in your room?"

"Yup, it's easier," Lanelle shrugged. "Tariana doesn't always get along with her roommate."

"Got it," Ayana replied. "Alright, I'll see y'all later."

With that, the two girls exchanged a wave before heading in separate directions. Ayana watched as Lanelle disappeared down the hall, her footsteps fading into the distance. The library's warm light dimmed as Ayana turned and made her way toward the exit, her thoughts already drifting to the upcoming plans and the growing connections she was making.

* * *

The pounding music still echoed faintly in Ayana's ears as she and Tariana walked toward the locker room, still catching their breath. The dance studio buzzed with chatter from the other girls on the team. Ayana noticed a few of them glancing her way as they walked past, some whispering to each other.

"You're getting noticed already," Tariana teased, nudging Ayana's shoulder.

"Noticed?" Ayana gave a skeptical look. "For what? Tripping on that last combo?"

"Girl, stop," Tariana laughed. "You did better than half of them out there. You know they're all sizing you up because you're new."

Ayana frowned. "Yeah, well, I'm not here for that. I just wanted to try something new, maybe meet some people."

"You definitely met people. And by the way, you might not care, but the captain does."

"Wait...the captain? What's her name again? Jade?"

"Yep," Tariana said, popping the "p." "And she's been running this team like her personal empire since second year. She's probably trying to figure out if you're competition or not."

"Competition?" Ayana echoed, rolling her eyes. "I've been

to one practice. I'm not trying to take anyone's spot."

"That's not how Jade sees it," Tariana warned. "You've got skills, and around here, that makes you a threat."

Ayana groaned and threw her head back dramatically. "Great. I didn't sign up for a dance team with high school politics."

"Welcome to extracurricular life," Tariana laughed. "But don't worry. As long as you stick with me, you're good. Jade doesn't mess with me—yet."

"Yet?"

"Let's just say I'm not exactly her favorite person," Tariana replied with a sly smile. "I may have...accidentally out shined her at last year's spring showcase."

"'Accidentally?'" Ayana raised an eyebrow.

"Okay, fine, maybe it was on purpose." Tariana laughed, flipping her ponytail. "But she deserved it. Girl doesn't like sharing the spotlight."

They entered the locker room, and the familiar scent of sweat and body spray hit Ayana's senses. Girls milled around, some swapping shoes, and wiping their faces with towels.

"Hey, Tariana," one of the girls—an athletic-looking redhead—called out. "Who's your friend?"

"This is Ayana," Tariana introduced proudly. "She's new, but y'all saw her out there killing it today."

Ayana waved shyly. "Hey."

The redhead nodded in approval. "You've got good footwork. Where'd you learn?"

"I just danced for fun. Never on a team," Ayana explained.

"Well, you kept up with us, and that's saying something," another girl chimed in, pulling her hair into a bun. "Jade's routines aren't easy."

Tariana crossed her arms and leaned casually against a row

of lockers. "Ayana's a natural."

"You think Jade noticed?" the redhead asked, lowering her voice.

"She notices everything," Tariana said, eyes narrowing slightly. "But don't worry about her. You've got me."

"I don't know whether to feel reassured or nervous," Ayana joked.

"Relax," Tariana grinned. "We've got your back."

After a quick change into street clothes, the two girls headed out of the building and toward the parking lot. The sun was starting to set, casting long shadows across the pavement. A group of students loitered near the front of the gym, including a tall girl with sleek black hair pulled into a high ponytail—Jade.

"Speak of the Devil," Tariana muttered under her breath. "Here we go."

Jade spotted them and sauntered over with two other girls following close behind. Her lips curved into a smile that didn't quite reach her eyes.

"Hey, Tariana," Jade greeted, her gaze sliding over to Ayana. "And you must be Ayana."

"Uh, yeah. Nice to meet you," Ayana said, trying to keep her tone neutral.

"You've got some moves," Jade said, crossing her arms. "First time on a team?"

Ayana nodded. "Yeah. I just wanted to try something different."

"Well, different is good," Jade said with a catty smile. "But you'll find that we take things pretty seriously around here. Consistency matters. Commitment matters. We have a reputation to uphold."

"Of course," Ayana said, meeting Jade's gaze evenly. "I

wouldn't be here if I wasn't serious."

"Good," Jade said, clearly testing her. "I'll be watching."

With that, she turned on her heel and walked away, her entourage following.

"Well, that was fun," Ayana muttered under her breath.

"Girl, you handled that like a pro," Tariana whistled. "Jade likes to size people up early. She probably wanted to see if you'd crumble."

"Crack under pressure? Please," Ayana scoffed. "I've got enough going on in my life. I'm not afraid of a dance captain."

"Good," Tariana said, clapping her on the back. "Because things just got real. Welcome to the team."

They laughed and headed toward the parking lot, the tension easing as the night breeze swept over them. Ayana felt a strange mix of exhilaration and anticipation. She hadn't expected to be thrown into the deep end so quickly, but maybe this was exactly what she needed.

Shadows of Deception

amien and Ayana stood at the entrance of the secret garden, its colors fading into muted shades of gray. Leaves drooped like wilted banners, and the once-luminous flowers crumbled. Everything felt suffocated, as though The Garden itself were holding its breath.

"This place feels worse every time," Ayana muttered, clutching her bag.

Damien scanned the paths ahead, his jaw tightening. "If we don't get to the core soon, there won't be anything left to save."

As they started walking, magic pulsed faintly beneath their feet, flickering in and out of existence like a dying heartbeat. They passed under an ancient archway, where words shimmered in faint silver light:

"To save the heart, first lose your way; Seek truth where shadows stray."

Damien ran his fingers over the inscription. "Lose our way? That doesn't sound reassuring."

Ayana raised an eyebrow. "When has anything about this place been straightforward? This is either a guide or another trick."

A deep, rumbling growl echoed through the forest. They

froze. Damien instinctively reached for his knife.

"You have a knife!" Ayana squeaked incredulously.

"Ana, Michael said this would be dangerous. I needed to come prepared."

The air rumbled again.

"Did you hear that?" Ayana whispered, her eyes darting through the shifting shadows.

"Yeah," Damien said grimly, scanning the trees. "And it's not friendly."

A massive, serpent-like creature slithered out from the underbrush. Its scales shimmered like obsidian, its eyes glowing with an eerie green light. It reared up, hissing, and flicked its forked tongue.

"Run!" Damien shouted, grabbing Ayana's hand. They sprinted down the twisting path, the serpent crashing through the foliage behind them.

"We're going the wrong way!" Ayana gasped, glancing back at the creature.

"Well, the riddle did say to lose our way!" Damien shot back.

Ahead, the path split into three directions. Damien yanked Ayana toward the middle path. She tripped over her feet and hit the ground.

"My knees," she cried out.

"There is no time," Damien shouted pulling her to her feet.

Ayana stumbled but managed to get upright. "What the hell is that thing? Some kind of mutant snake?"

"Something worse," Damien said grimly. "It's part of the magic protecting this place."

The serpent hissed, its massive body weaving through the trees like a shadow. Leaves crumbled as it surged forward, splitting one of the ancient trees in half with a crushing snap of its body.

"We can't outrun it forever," Ayana said, clutching her side.

Damien nodded, his mind racing for a plan. "Alright, listen. If this thing's part of The Garden's defense, we need to outsmart it, not outrun it."

Ayana wiped the sweat from her brow. "How do you propose we outsmart a snake that's built like a tank and can smell fear?"

"We use deception," Damien replied, his voice steady. "It's too focused on us. Let's give it something else to focus on."

The serpent slithered closer,. Damien tightened his grip on his knife and glanced around. The ground beneath them was soft, littered with scattered vines and dense foliage.

"Ayana, remember those vines we passed earlier?" he asked.

"Yeah...?" Ayana replied, confused.

"Find some of the thickest ones you can and loop them over that branch," Damien pointed to a tree with a low-hanging sturdy limb. "We're going to set a trap."

Ayana sprinted toward the nearest cluster of vines while Damien shouted and waved his arms to draw the serpent's attention. "Hey! Over here, you ugly thing! Is that all you got?"

The serpent hissed furiously and lunged at him. Damien rolled out of the way, narrowly avoiding its snapping jaws. The ground shook as the creature slammed into the spot where he had been standing moments before.

"Got it!" Ayana yelled, dragging a bundle of thick vines behind her. Quickly, she began looping them over the tree branch as Damien led the serpent in a wide circle around the clearing.

"Hurry Ayana!" he called out, dodging another strike. His boots skidded across the damp soil as he barely escaped the serpent's reach.

"Almost...done!" Ayana grunted as she tied the last knot, anchoring the vines securely to a hidden boulder in the under-growth. "It's ready!"

Damien sprinted toward her, leading the serpent into the trap's path. The massive creature followed, its movements growing more frenzied as it sensed the trickery. Just as the serpent lunged again, Damien grabbed Ayana's arm and pulled her behind the boulder.

"Now!" Damien shouted.

Ayana kicked the release vine with all her strength. The tree branch snapped upright, yanking the tangled vines taut. The serpent jerked back, its head suddenly caught in the snare. It thrashed violently, trying to free itself, but the more it struggled, the tighter the vines held.

"Holy shit, it worked," Ayana breathed, staring at the serpent as it writhed and hissed.

"Don't celebrate just yet," Damien huffed. "We need to find the next clue and get out of here before it breaks loose."

They hurried past the trapped creature, deeper into the overgrown path. The serpent's enraged cries echoed behind them as they stumbled upon a large stone pedestal covered in runes.

"This has to be it," Damien said, tracing his fingers over the glowing symbols. The runes pulsed softly under his touch.

Ayana leaned closer. "Look at this—'*Only when shadows dance and truth is lost will the heart be revealed.*' What does that even mean?"

"It's another riddle," Damien muttered in frustration. "We don't have time for this."

A loud crack echoed through the forest. They turned to see

the serpent thrashing more violently, the vines straining under its immense strength.

"Damien," Ayana said nervously. "It's getting free."

Damien clenched his jaw. "We can't solve this right now. Let's head back and regroup. We'll figure it out with fresh eyes."

Ayana nodded. "Yeah, good idea. I don't want to be snake food."

They backed away from the pedestal, taking one last glance at the cryptic runes before turning toward the path leading out of the clearing. The serpent's hisses grew louder, but the trap still held—for now.

They sprinted through the twisting paths, following the trail of markers they had left earlier. The trees seemed to close in on them, the dense shadows stretching like grasping hands. Finally, they burst through the thick foliage and into the open field near the entrance of the secret garden.

Ayana bent over, hands on her knees, catching her breath. "Okay...that was too close."

Damien nodded, sucking in air. "We made it out. That's what matters."

"But we still don't have all the answers," Ayana said, straightening up. "This garden is throwing riddles and monsters at us like it's testing us or something."

"Maybe it is," Damien said thoughtfully. "But we'll come back. Next time, we'll be ready."

They walked away from The Garden's fading entrance, the weight of their unfinished quest hanging heavily over them. The Garden's secrets weren't going to be easy to unlock—but neither of them had any intention of giving up.

* * *

Back on campus, Ayana hurried to her room to grab her things. She had to make it to Lanelle's room for the study session. These sessions had really helped her stay on track.

"What's the rush?" Damien asked, leaning against the doorframe.

"I've got to get to Lanelle's for study night. You should come," Ayana said, glancing back at him as she gathered her belongings.

"Nah, I'm good," Damien replied, shrugging.

"Are you hanging out with Dion and the others?" she asked.

Damien didn't respond right away.

Ayana narrowed her eyes as she stepped inside her room. "Hello? Earth to Damien," she prompted.

He sighed and ran a hand over his head. "We've just been meeting up to show me around and walk me to classes."

"That's all? Have you checked out basketball or anything else?" she asked, continuing to toss things into her bag.

Damien stayed silent. Ayana sucked her teeth in frustration.

"Look, I've jumped in headfirst—book club, dance, study groups. I'm not saying you have to be best friends with everyone here, but don't leave me to figure this all out by myself," she said, giving him a pointed look.

Damien exhaled heavily. "Alright, alright. I hear you."

"I'll text you when I get back here okay?" Ayana said without waiting for an answer. "Shut my door," she yelled behind her.

Lanelle's dorm room was cozy, the scent of lavender wafting from a nearby candle. The walls were decorated with photos and string lights. Textbooks, notes, highlighters, and snacks were spread out around them. Ayana sat cross-legged on the bed, flipping through her book. Tariana sprawled out on the floor, leaning back against the bed frame, while Lanelle sat at her desk, pretending to concentrate on her notes.

"So," Tariana started. "We going to talk about Booker or what?" she asked.

Lanelle didn't look up from her computer.

"Alright, Lanelle," Tariana started, raising an eyebrow dramatically. "So let me get this straight. Booker's out here breaking hearts and keeping secrets, and Jalen's over there like Prince Charming, waiting for you to notice him. Girl, are you starring in a *Lifetime* movie and forgot to tell us?"

Lanelle groaned and covered her face. "Oh my God, Tariana. It is not even like that!"

"How is it like then?" Tariana asked. "This is premium drama material! I mean, you've got the 'guy-who-hurt-me-but-wants-redemption' arc and the 'new-guy-who's-secretly-perfect' subplot. I'm over here waiting for the dramatic showdown where Jalen and Booker fight in the rain or something."

Ayana burst into laughter, nearly dropping her textbook.

"I call it coping with humor," Tariana smirked. "Someone has to bring the comic relief. Otherwise, we'll all end up in therapy. Speaking of which, Lanelle, you might want to charge these boys for the emotional labor you're putting in."

"Tariana!" Lanelle choked out, half-laughing, half-shocked. "I cannot with you."

Tariana grinned wider and wagged her finger. "Nah, girl, I'm serious. You're out here trying to heal from betrayal and still pulling straight A's. Meanwhile, Booker's probably struggling to pass his combat. You're the real MVP."

Ayana chuckled and shook her head. "She's got a point.

You're holding it together pretty damn well, considering everything. I didn't know all this was going on."

Lanelle leaned back in her chair and sighed, though a smile crept onto her face. "You two are too much. I can't even wallow in peace."

"Wallowing is overrated," Tariana said, tossing a highlighter onto Lanelle's desk. "You've got two cute guys fighting for your attention. The least you can do is embrace the chaos. Hell, I'd be living my best life right now."

"Yeah, right," Ayana teased. "You'd probably have them doing your homework and fetching you coffee."

"Exactly!" Tariana said with mock seriousness. "You gotta set the standards high. Booker wants to earn your trust back? Cool. Tell him to learn how to cook and deliver a full-course meal. Jalen's being sweet? That's great. He can serenade you with a violin. I need both effort and entertainment value."

Lanelle laughed, the tension in her chest easing with each joke. "You're insane, you know that?"

"Insanely right," Tariana shot back. "But for real, we're here for you. And if things get too messy, just say the word and I'll handle it. I'm not above a little 'accidental' tripping in the hallway if Booker steps out of line again."

Lanelle snorted. "You'd trip him and then blame gravity."

"Damn right I would," Tariana said, crossing her arms proudly. "Gravity works in mysterious ways."

Lanelle shook her head, laughter bubbling from her throat. "Okay, okay, you win. No more serious vibes tonight. I'll take things one step at a time, and you two can keep being my chaotic support system."

"That's all we needed to hear," Tariana said, giving Lanelle a playful salute. "Now, let's get back to studying before Ayana has a breakdown over this covert work."

"Too late," Ayana muttered, flipping a page. "I'm already one bad grade away from losing my mind."

"Well, at least you're not one bad secret away from a campus scandal," Tariana quipped.

"Tariana!" Lanelle shouted, laughing harder.

The room filled with their laughter. The girls settled back into their study session, but the warmth of friendship and humor lingered, making the night a little brighter.

Balls in the Air - Secrets Everywhere

amien sat on a bench near the campus quad, earbuds in, but no music playing. Around him, students laughed, talked, and moved in clusters, their easy camaraderie reminding him of everything he didn't have here. It wasn't that he hadn't tried. People were friendly enough, but nothing had really clicked.

He scrolled through his phone absentmindedly until a message popped up from Dion.

Yo, we're at the rec center. Come through.

Damien stared at the message for a moment. He hadn't made much of an effort to hang out with them. Maybe that was his problem. With a sigh, he typed out a reply.

On my way.

Pocketing his phone, Damien stood and made his way toward the rec center. It was time to stop sulking and do something about the loneliness.

The rec center was buzzing. Sneakers squeaked against the gym floor and basketballs hit the rims echoed through the large space. Damien spotted Dion, Quashawn and Booker on the court. Dion and Booker engaged in a fast-paced game of one-on-one. Dion saw him first, waving him over.

"Finally decided to show up, huh?" Dion teased as he passed

the ball to Booker.

"Yeah," Damien said, walking onto the court. "Figured I'd stop being a hermit."

"About time," Booker added, dribbling the ball with ease. "We were starting to think you were allergic to fun."

Damien chuckled. "Nah, just trying to get used to everything."

"Well, now you're here," Dion said, passing Damien the ball. "Let's see if you've got any game."

Damien dribbled a few times and took a shot. The ball bounced off the rim, and Booker grabbed the rebound effortlessly.

"Man, you've got to work on that form," Booker smirked.

"Yeah, yeah," Damien muttered, shaking his head. "Let me warm up."

They played a few rounds of half-court, the game light and competitive. Dion's trash talk kept the energy high, while Booker's steady, focused play balanced it out. Damien found himself laughing more than he had in weeks. Slowly, the tension in his chest began to ease.

"That was your shot?" Dion mocked after Damien missed a jump shot. "Man, even Lanelle's got better range than that, and she doesn't even play."

"Oh, here we go," Damien muttered, wiping sweat from his brow. "Maybe if someone passed the ball instead of running their mouth, I'd get some practice in."

"Sounds like excuses to me," Dion quipped. "Booker, tell this man he's trash."

Booker laughed. "I'm not getting involved. You two can argue all you want."

After a few more rounds, they called it quits and sat on the sidelines, cooling off with bottles of water. Damien leaned back, enjoying the break.

"So," Dion said, wiping sweat from his face. "You and Ayana seem pretty solid. How's that going?"

"Good," Damien said with a nod. "She's amazing. She pushed me to get involved more. If it weren't for her, I'd probably still be sitting in my dorm binge-watching shows."

"She's right. Deceptive's like its own city. You've got to get involved," Dion said with a grin.

"Appreciate that," Damien replied. "What about you two? You've known each other forever, right?"

"Naw, we just met last year. We stayed cool after all that happened," Dion replied.

"What happened last year?"

Dion and Booker exchanged a look. Booker's expression darkened slightly, and Dion leaned forward, resting his elbows on his knees.

"Lanelle and Booker were tight last semester," Dion explained. "Like, real tight. dating tight. But then…"

"Then I screwed up," Booker interrupted. He rubbed the back of his neck, clearly uncomfortable. "Things got messy with my biological father and the twins. I messed up."

Damien frowned. "Your biological father? What does that have to do with anything?"

Booker sighed. "It's just a whole mess. I was…I was supposed to keep tabs on the twins for him, especially Lanelle. He wanted information about them, but I never wanted to get them involved in any of that."

Damien's eyes widened. "You were spying on them?"

"Not exactly," Booker said quickly, shaking his head. "At first, I didn't know what I was walking into. Then I got stuck. I was torn between doing what he wanted and protecting them. I didn't tell Lanelle. When she found out…let's just say things haven't been the same since."

"Damn," Damien muttered. "No wonder she's upset. That's a huge betrayal."

"Yeah," Dion said, crossing his arms. "I mean, I understood eventually, but Lanelle's big on trust. Once you break it, good luck getting it back."

Damien nodded slowly. "That's rough. Trust is hard to get back once it's broken."

"Tell me about it," Booker muttered. "I've been trying to make it right ever since, but it's like there's always this wall between us now. And then there's Jalen…"

"Jalen's been hanging around Lanelle a lot," Damien said. "I've noticed."

"Yeah, he's been trying to swoop in since the fallout," Dion smirked. "Dude's smooth, I'll give him that. But Lanelle's not the type to jump from one guy to another. She's still figuring out who she can trust."

Booker's jaw tightened. "I'm not mad at Jalen. He's been there for her when I wasn't. But yeah, it's hard watching from the sidelines."

Damien thought for a moment. "Sounds like a lot of unre-solved stuff. But hey, at least you're still trying. That's more than most people would do."

Booker gave a small nod. "Thanks, man."

Dion crossed his arms. "Still, bro, you've got to be prepared. Lanelle's not the type to let things slide. She's all about people proving themselves. You keep showing up, though—she'll see it eventually."

"I hope so," Booker replied quietly.

Damien chuckled, trying to lighten the mood. "Man, this is turning into a full-blown soap opera. You're telling me people really keep up with all this drama?"

"Welcome to Deceptive High," Dion said, throwing his arms up theatrically. "It's more entertaining than anything on Netflix."

The three of them burst into laughter. Damien leaned back and for the first time in a while, felt a part of something real.

II

Lies, Laughs, and Limelight

Mark, Tiff, and Twisted Tea

Tariana and Ayana glistened with sweat as they emerged from dance practice.

"Where you headed?" Tariana asked Ayana.

"Girl, I am going to my room. I am so gross. I need to soak the sore away."

"You've been doing good," Tariana encouraged.

Ayana had been keeping up, making little mistakes, and taking no prisoners. But she was the only new person on the team. Everyone else had been there for a year already. Plus, she went from sometimes activity to full-blown sport and her body felt it.

"I don't want to give Jade a reason to kick me off. But my body is feeling it," she said. "What you got going on?" she asked.

Tariana was distracted by someone calling her name. Jade was coming at them.

"Hold up a minute," she yelled.

They looked at each other quizzically and stood waiting for Jade.

"Look," she said shoving her phone at them.

Tariana looked up at Jade. "Are we doing it?" she asked.

"Hell yeah, we are and we aren't going to be the only dance team. I got this from Mark who heard his girl Tiff saying she and her girls were dancing."

Tariana scrunched up her face like she smelled something foul.

"Who's Mark and Tiff?" Ayana asked.

"I'll fill you in later," Tariana said and turned back to Jade.

"We will be adding three more practices this week," Jade said. "But we don't have this space so we have to meet in the gym."

"Okay," the girls said in unison.

Jade looked at Ayana, eyes narrowed. "You ready?"

"Absolutely," she said more confident than she felt.

With one last look, Jade turned and left.

As the girls walked back through campus, the quad lights cast long shadows on the pathways. "So, you were saying about Mark and Tiff?" Ayana prompted, curiosity getting the better of her.

Tariana scoffed and launched into the juicy backstory. "Mark and Tiffany are a hot mess. They've been on again, off again. During one of their 'off' phases, Mark started dating Jade."

Ayana's eyes widened. "Dang, so Jade swooped in and stole Mark away from Tiff??"

Tariana gave a loud, exaggerated suck of her teeth. "Girl, no. Everyone knows Mark and Tiff's relationship is like bad Wi-Fi—unstable. Jade should've known better than to even get involved."

Ayana wrinkled her nose. "But if Mark and Tiff are so messy, why does Jade still talk to him?"

Tariana smirked knowingly. "Oh, they still talk. And then some."

Ayana gave her a pointed look. "You're holding out on me."

Tariana cackled and waved her hand dismissively. "The rest is not my business, honey. I'm not about to end up in their soap opera."

"Oh my God," Ayana groaned, shaking her head in disbelief. "Drama just follows some people, huh?"

Tariana's phone buzzed, interrupting them. She pulled it out and squinted at the screen. "Hold up, the group chat is popping off," she said, her thumbs flying over the keyboard.

"Let me guess—more nonsense?" Ayana teased.

"Nonsense and snacks, probably," Tariana shot back with a laugh. They continued walking, the night air carrying their laughter across the quiet campus paths.

Dion: Yo, y'all ready for the talent show Friday? 🎤🎵⭐

Lanelle: I'm thinking about it… not really sure what to do yet.

Booker: Lanelle, you gotta sing over one of my beats! I've got something perfect for you. 🎧🌐

Lanelle: 👀 Really, Booker? You know I'm not trying to put myself out there like that.

Booker: C'mon, Nell. It's fire. You'll crush it, I promise. We'd kill it together. ✨

Tariana: Oooohhh, *yes*! Do it, Nelly! I'll hype you from the front row. 😁 Also, speaking of hype, the dance team is doing a whole set! Me and Ayana going to kill it.💃✨

Quashawn: Oh great, so more excuses to make us sit through endless rehearsals, huh?

Tariana: Boy, I know you're not talking. You're the one who begged to be in the routine this year.

Quashawn: OKAY. But y'all take practice way too seriously. We're not competing for Olympic gold here. 🥇

Dion: Bruh, you better not mess up the routine this time. Last year, you almost took Tariana out with that "creative freestyle."

Quashawn: That was ONE time, Dion. One! Let it go already. 😬

Lanelle: LOL y'all are wild.

Booker: Sooooo... about that beat, Nell. You in? 🔊

Lanelle: Ugh. Look, Booker... we're still not cool, okay? You know that. I'm not exactly jumping at the chance to work with you.

Booker: I get that. I messed up. But can we at least try to make something awesome together? One performance. No strings attached.

Tariana: *Nelly...* C'mon, girl. You're not about to pass this up, are you?

Lanelle: Fine. I'll come listen to it. But I'm not making any promises. If I hate it, you're on your own.

Booker: Deal. You won't regret it.

Tariana: This is going to be epic. We're about to make history at Deceptive High. 🎉✨

Dion: Facts. Let's all bring the heat Friday night! 🔆

Quashawn: I'm just here for the post-show snacks, tbh. 🍪

Lanelle: SMH. Priorities, Quashawn.

Tariana: Don't worry. He'll be too tired to snack after all the dancing I've got planned for him.

Quashawn: Pray for me.

Tariana finally looked up from her phone.

"We need to get you in the group chat girl," Tariana said.

She went back to tapping on her phone and then Ayana got a ping on her phone.

Tariana: Oh, by the way, I added Ayana to the group chat. She's gonna be part of the dance team performance! 🤸✨

Ayana: Hey, everyone! 👋 Thanks for the add, Tariana.

Dion: Let me add Damien too. He's coming to hang with us at the show.

Damien: What up, y'all! I'm not dancing though. I'm just here for moral support... and the food. 🍔🍽️

Quashawn: Finally, someone who gets it!

Tariana: Y'all are hopeless. Anyway, who's down for a group dinner? We haven't all eat together in a while. 🌑✧

Dion: For sure.

Booker: I'm in.

Lanelle: Yeah, I'm down.

Ayana: Sounds great! I can definitely eat after practice.

Damien: Alright then, it's a plan.

Tariana: Yes! Okay, crew.

Quashawn: Just make sure there's dessert.

Lanelle: SMH, Quashawn. Priorities, man.

The girls giggled and continued chatting until they reached the bend to part ways. "Hit me up after practice tomorrow," Tariana called over her shoulder.

"You know I will!" Ayana replied with a grin before turning toward her dorm. Her legs felt heavier with each step as she thought about food, homework, and the bliss of a long shower. The cool night air brushed her face, momentarily soothing her aching muscles. Just as she reached the entrance to Mitchell Hall, her phone buzzed with a text from Damien.

Damien: Hey, I'm at your room. Let's catch up.

Ayana picked up her pace, climbing the dorm stairs two at a time. When she opened the door to her room, Damien was sitting casually on her bed, laughing with her roommate, Mary. His relaxed posture contrasted with the alertness in her mind as she processed the scene.

"Well, hello," Ayana said, crossing her arms and arching an eyebrow.

Damien raised a hand defensively. "Mary let me in," he explained.

Mary grinned, bouncing slightly on her bed. "I barely see

you guys! It's like we're in different time zones. I was excited to finally catch you here. I've been spending way too much time over in Spencer's room. It's like my second home at this point."

Ayana gave a slow, drawn-out "Ohhkayy". "Sounds like you're practically moved in with Spencer. You'd better not be charging rent."

Mary laughed and threw a pillow at Ayana. "Please, if anyone should be paying rent, it's Spencer. I'm his unofficial life coach now."

Ayana caught the pillow and tossed it back. "You're doing the Lord's work," she teased before turning to Damien. "So, you're hanging with Dion, Booker, and Quashawn?"

"Yeah. I joined the basketball team with them. Took your advice," Damien said with a smirk.

Ayana tilted her head proudly. "Well, thank you for listening. It's about time you took some of my advice."

Damien smirked. "Hey, every now and then, you have good ideas."

"See? Proof that you're a positive influence," Mary interjected and gave Ayana a playful thumbs-up.

"What about food?" Damien asked. "Remember you need to nurture your body."

Ayana sighed dramatically. "Fine. You grab something while I shower. But make it quick—I don't want cold fries or stale pizza. We'll eat and do homework together."

"Deal," Damien agreed.

As Ayana grabbed her towel and shower caddy, Mary chimed in again. "Hey, if he forgets dessert, make sure you kick him out. Priorities, girl."

Ayana chuckled. "Oh, he's on thin ice already. Don't worry,

Mary. I'll keep him in check."

"Wow, no pressure at all," Damien quipped, holding up his hands.

"None," Ayana shot back. "Don't slack. I'm holding you to that food run," she added with a mock-serious glare.

"Yes, ma'am," Damien replied, giving her a playful salute.

Ayana chuckled softly as she headed toward the shower, silently thanking the universe for the rare luxury of Lanelle's single dorm—complete with its own private bathroom. The thought of hot water washing away the day's soreness was the perfect motivator.

Layups, Lineups, and Loaded Stories

The echo of sneakers on polished wood filled the gym as Coach Reynolds blew his whistle. "Alright, listen up! We're running the defensive drill again," he barked, pacing along the sideline. Every player straightened up in response.

Dion wiped sweat from his forehead, exchanging a glance with Booker. "Man, Coach isn't playing today," he muttered.

"Good. We need this," Booker replied, adjusting his head-band.

"Damien! Get in position!" Coach Reynolds shouted. Damien nodded, jogging to the top of the key.

"All right, defense, I want you to lock them down! Offense, move the ball fast—no lazy passes!" Coach continued.

The whistle shrieked, and the drill began. Booker dribbled down the court, eyes darting for an opening. Dion sprinted to the wing, raising his hand for the ball. Damien was on him in a flash, cutting off his lane.

"Keep the pressure! Don't let him breathe!" Coach yelled.

Booker hesitated, then faked a pass to the corner before driving to the basket. Damien shifted quickly, his arms outstretched to block, but Booker twisted midair and flipped the ball back to Dion.

Dion took a quick shot from the three-point line. The ball clanged off the rim, and chaos erupted under the basket as players scrambled for the rebound.

"Box out! Box out!" Coach barked.

Damien muscled his way inside, snatching the ball, and pushing it down the court in a fast break. He darted past two defenders and laid it in with a smooth finger roll.

"Nice hustle!" Coach Reynolds called out, nodding approvingly.

The team reset, panting but determined. Quashawn, who had been watching from the sideline, jogged onto the court when Coach waved him in.

"Let's go, Quashawn. Show me you've got some fire today," Coach said with a grin.

"Oh, I got this, Coach," Quashawn replied, cracking his neck dramatically.

"Yeah, yeah. Prove it," Damien teased as he took his position on defense.

The whistle blew again, and Quashawn caught the inbound pass. He drove forward with surprising speed, crossing over and pulling up for a jumper just outside the paint. The ball swished through the net.

"Okay, okay!" Dion shouted, laughing. "Looks like somebody actually came to play!"

"Don't let it get to your head," Booker smirked.

"Focus!" Coach Reynolds interrupted, his voice cutting through the banter. "This is practice, not a trash-talk session. Keep moving!"

The drill continued. Players called out screens and switches, their voices blending with the squeak of shoes and the rhythmic bounce of the ball. Every play was met with either praise or correction from Coach Reynolds.

"Quashawn, follow through on your shot next time!"

"Damien, good footwork on defense!"

"Dion, stop hesitating—take the shot when you have it!"

By the end of the session, the players were dripping with sweat and breathing heavily. Coach blew the whistle one last time.

"Alright, bring it in!" he commanded. The team gathered, forming a tight circle around him. "You guys worked hard today. This is the kind of effort I want to see every practice. Keep pushing, and we'll dominate at the next game. Got it?"

"Yes, Coach!" the team shouted in unison.

"Good. Hit the showers. And don't forget—team meeting tomorrow at 6:30 sharp. Don't be late!"

The players broke the huddle, exchanging fist bumps and high-fives. As they headed off the court, Quashawn jogged up beside Damien.

"See? I told you I'd bring the heat," Quashawn said with a grin.

"Man, one shot doesn't make you a legend," Damien retorted.

"Just wait till the next practice," Quashawn shot back.

"Yeah, yeah. We'll see," Dion added, throwing an arm around both of them as they made their way to the locker room.

The locker room buzzed with the aftermath of a grueling basketball practice. Overhead lights flickered slightly, casting a harsh glow on the rows of dented, scratched, and chipped blue lockers. The scent of sweat and worn rubber filled the humid air, mingled with the faint trace of disinfectant.

Players shuffled in, some still catching their breath, others wiping their faces with damp towels. Damien peeled off his jersey, his muscles glistening under the bright lights. He tossed the shirt onto a nearby bench with a loud slap. "Man, Coach was pushing us today," he muttered, grabbing a bottle of water and taking a long gulp.

"Pushing? That's putting it mildly," Dion replied, collapsing onto the bench with a heavy sigh. He began untying his sneakers, grimacing as his legs cramped. "I'm feeling every single one of those fast breaks."

"You're not the only one," Quashawn added, toweling off his face. He leaned against his locker, grinning despite the exhaustion. "But hey, I made y'all look bad with that shot earlier. Admit it."

Damien laughed. "Bruh, you hit one shot. You're not exactly MVP."

"Give him his moment," Booker chimed in, lacing up a fresh pair of slides. "It'll keep him quiet for five minutes."

"Y'all haters," Quashawn shot back, shaking his head.

Slamming lockers and dripping shower water filled the room. A few players crowded around a speaker blasting low hip-hop beats, nodding their heads in unison. Others traded stories about the toughest drills from practice, each tale growing more exaggerated with each retelling.

"You guys ready for the crew dinner tonight?" Dion asked.

"Hell yeah," Booker replied, grabbing his duffel bag. "I'm not showing up late again like last time. I'm getting the good stuff first."

"Don't blame the food; blame your slow ass," Damien teased.

Laughter echoed off the tiled walls as they began to pack up. Despite the exhaustion, there was more excitement for the next game.

* * *

The guys entered the cafeteria and looked around for the girls.

"Ain't no way we beat them here," Dion said as he scanned the room.

As they peered around the crowded room, Damien spotted Ayana. "There's Ana," he said, nodding toward the back.

They followed his lead, weaving through the students and staggered tables, until they reached a room tucked at the rear of the cafeteria. Dion stepped inside and paused, glancing around.

"What is this place?" he asked.

Tariana turned, her face lighting up with a smile as she held her arms out wide. "Surprise," she said.

Lanelle chuckled. "Tariana is dating the guy who works under events and catering. He gave us the room because it's so many of us. Kasa and Deslin are coming too."

Quashawn furrowed his brow. "Dating?" he questioned, eyes narrowing suspiciously.

Tariana glared at Lanelle. "Mind your business, Dad," she drawled, crossing her arms.

Lanelle held up her hands with a mischievous grin. "I'm just saying, and we are not dating."

"Uh-huh. That's what it looked like earlier," Ayana added with a teasing smirk.

Tariana's head snapped toward Ayana. "Traitor," she accused.

"So, you do have a boyfriend," Quashawn teased as the guys made their way to the table.

Imani tossed her bag on the bench beside Dion. "What's all this talk about Tariana having a boyfriend?" she asked.

As the conversations around the table grew, Imani leaned toward Ayana. "So, how's dance practice going? Jade still working y'all to death?"

Ayana chuckled. "You have no idea. My muscles are staging a full rebellion."

"Oh, I believe it," Imani said with a smirk. "Back when I was on the team, Jade made me question my life choices every other practice. Just wait—she'll probably throw in extra sessions right before the talent show."

"Don't jinx it!" Ayana groaned, shaking her head.

"Don't listen to them. They're just nosy," Tariana retorted, giving Lanelle and Quashawn a pointed look.

"I'm with you on that one," Imani said, laughing as she sat beside Dion. "But for real, Tariana, this setup looks amazing."

Tariana had transformed the usually dull room with a clean white tablecloth she'd borrowed from the kitchen staff. At the center, she placed a small, simple bouquet of bright wildflowers she'd picked from around campus. Battery-operated tea lights surrounded the arrangement, casting a warm, inviting glow that softened the cafeteria's harsh fluorescent lighting. She had even arranged the plates, napkins, and utensils neatly, giving the space an unexpectedly elegant touch.

"Dang, Tariana. You really turned this into a five-star experience," Dion said, plopping into his seat.

"Five stars on a budget," Tariana quipped, adjusting one of the tea lights.

"A budget of free," Lanelle muttered under her breath.

"It's cozy," Ayana said as she took her seat. "Better than what we're used to, that's for sure."

"Thank you! Now y'all better appreciate this," Tariana replied, waving her hand dramatically. "It's not easy keeping things classy in a cafeteria."

"No Jalen?" Dion asked as Kasa and Deslin walked in, greeting everyone.

He glanced at Booker and shrugged. "I mean, since Kasa and D are here and all," he clarified.

"He couldn't make it," Lanelle replied, trying to appear nonchalant but looking down at her phone. "I asked."

Once everyone had grabbed their food, the table came alive with conversation, laughter, and clinking utensils. The atmosphere was warm and buzzing with energy. Conversations overlapped and crisscrossed in every direction.

Lanelle and Booker leaned in close, quietly discussing music arrangements for the talent show. Booker tapped rhythms on the table. "The beat I made has this slow build. You'll love it, just trust me," he said. Lanelle hesitated but nodded. "Fine, but if it's corny, I'm walking off stage."

On the other side of the table, Dion and Damien were locked in a heated debate about basketball plays. "Bro, I'm telling you, you're not aggressive enough on fast breaks," Dion said, waving a fork in the air for emphasis.

"Nah, you just wanna run like it's a marathon every possession," Damien shot back, shaking his head as he took a bite of his burger. "Efficiency, man. Efficiency."

"Yeah, because that's why you missed that layup in practice?" Quashawn chimed in.

"Keep talking, Quashawn, and I'll dunk on you tomorrow," Damien retorted, narrowing his eyes.

Meanwhile, Tariana and Kasa were reminiscing about last year's talent show mishaps. "Remember when that guy tried to juggle flaming batons and almost burned down the stage?" Kasa asked, giggling.

"Girl, how could I forget? The fire alarm went off, and we had to evacuate!" Tariana added, shaking her head.

Deslin, usually quiet, chimed in. "I heard they banned fire acts after that."

"Smart move," Ayana muttered between bites. She was half-listening while texting Ryan, her sister, to update her on the day's events. Across from her, Damien caught her eye and raised an eyebrow. "Everything good?"

"Yeah, just catching up with my sis," she replied.

The conversations continued, the energy rising and falling like waves. People traded food, with Quashawn stealing a fry from Dion's plate and narrowly dodging a napkin missile in retaliation. Tariana, ever the organizer, kept the flow of conversation moving, making sure everyone was included.

"You know, this might be the calm before the storm," Lanelle said, glancing around the table.

"Storm?" Dion asked, raising an eyebrow.

"Yeah," she replied. "Talent shows always bring drama. Just wait."

"Good thing we have snacks to survive it," Quashawn joked, earning a chorus of laughter from the group.

For that moment, all worries about practice, performances, and schoolwork faded. The group was in their element—bonded by shared experiences, stories, and the anticipation of the upcoming talent show. The night stretched on, filled with warmth, laughter, and the kind of camaraderie that only comes from moments like these.

Flame vs. Frost: The Remix

Lanelle and Booker spent a lot of time together over the past few days, working tirelessly on music and lyrics for their talent show performance. Between honing her skills with Dion, swimming practice, and keeping up with her classes, Lanelle felt like she was constantly on the move. Yet, there was something comforting about these sessions with Booker. Maybe it was the rare chance to sit still for a change. Or maybe...maybe it was because of him. She bit her lip, pushing the thought to the back of her mind.

They were in Booker's dorm room, which smelled faintly of vanilla air freshener and worn-out sneakers. A string of LED lights bathed the walls in a soft, ambient glow, and his computer screen reflected off the window, flickering with audio tracks. Booker lay sprawled across his bed, laptop balanced on his stomach, as he mixed beats and adjusted audio levels with a focused expression.

Lanelle sat cross-legged on a beanbag chair, her notebook and pencil resting on her knees. Her foot tapped lightly to the beat. They'd already nailed the chorus and two solid verses, but the bridge was harder. The frustration was starting to show in Booker's furrowed brow.

"Let me hear what you got," Lanelle suggested, breaking the

silence.

Booker sighed and clicked a few keys, rewinding the track. "It's almost there, but this one part...I don't know. It's not flowing how I want it to."

"Play it anyway. Maybe I can help."

The track started from the last chorus, rolling smoothly into the bridge. Lanelle bobbed her head in time with the rhythm, tapping her pencil on the edge of her notebook. As the music progressed, a heavier blend of drums, keyboard, and saxophone entered. She hummed along with the melody, her ears pricking as the saxophone riff fought to be heard beneath the other instruments.

When the track ended, she leaned forward. "What if you switched it up?"

Booker tilted his head. "Switched what?"

"The balance," she said, gesturing with her pencil. "Make the instruments stand out more. Especially the saxophone. That's my favorite instrument, and I want to actually hear it."

Booker's lips curled into a thoughtful smile. "You want me to bring the sax front and center?"

"Exactly. Let it shine. Right now, it's kind of getting lost under the beat."

"Okay, okay, I see where you're going," he said, already tapping at his keyboard to adjust the audio levels. "You're onto something."

As he worked, Lanelle watched him more than the screen. The way his brow furrowed in concentration, how he muttered under his breath when something didn't sound quite right. It was strangely endearing—but she quickly shook the thought away, focusing back on her notebook.

The new version of the track started to play. This time, the saxophone rose above the other elements, smooth and soulful. Lanelle closed her eyes, letting the sound wash over her. A grin tugged at her lips.

"Now that's what I'm talking about," she said, snapping her fingers. "It's got character now."

Booker chuckled softly. "Good call. You've got an ear for this."

"I've got ears for a lot of things," she teased, flashing him a playful smile. "But don't get cocky. We're not done yet."

"Yes, ma'am," he replied with a mock salute. "Let's hit this bridge and make it perfect."

As they continued collaborating, the tension eased into laughter and light banter. In that moment, the outside world faded. It was just the two of them, the music, and the shared drive to create something unforgettable.

"Okay, okay, let's practice for real. One time through before Dion shows up," Booker said.

Lanelle was sprawled out on Booker's bed, looking at the ceiling. She lifted her head to look at Booker when the music didn't start. "Come on," she said.

"Stand up, please?" he asked pointedly.

Lanelle sucked her teeth. "Ugh, fine."

"Come on, Lanelle, let's do this one for real. Friday is in two days."

Lanelle shuffled out of the bed and stood. Booker started the beat and she began singing.

At the end of the song, they both hooted in elation.

"That's what I am talking about," Booker said.

Lanelle laughed and, without thinking, she threw herself into his arms for a hug. The moment stretched—too long. Awareness crept in, and she pulled away, clearing her throat.

"So um, I'll get this to the people right away."

"You got to be up there on stage with me," she insisted. "Can't you hook up your computer or something and play it like a DJ?"

He shrugged. "I can ask."

Silence fell between them, heavy with something unspoken. Booker shifted, rubbing the back of his neck. "Lanelle...I'm really sorry. For everything I did."

Lanelle inhaled sharply, then exhaled slowly. She nodded. "I hear you...I just don't know what to say."

Booker hesitated, then blurted out, "Are you and Jalen...a thing?"

Lanelle blinked, caught off guard. "What?"

"You and Jalen," Booker said, his tone careful but laced with something deeper—something vulnerable. "You guys seemed close. I don't know, I just...wondered."

Lanelle frowned, crossing her arms. "We talk. We're friends."

"Right." Booker nodded, looking down. "I mean, I know it's none of my business. Just... forget I said anything."

Lanelle studied him, the way he suddenly wouldn't meet her eyes. "Speak your mind, Booker."

Booker scoffed. "Nah, it's just...Jalen always seemed like the type to have everything figured out. And I—" He shook his head, exhaling in frustration. "Never mind."

Lanelle softened. "Booker."

He forced a grin. "It's cool, Lanelle. Like I said, forget it."

As she grabbed her belongings and turned to leave, she felt that same tension hanging in the air, thick with everything still left unsaid.

She looked back at him and shrugged before walking out the

door, leaving him staring after her, lost in his own thoughts.

* * *

Dion came into the room loud arguing with Imani.

"I'm just saying, Dion. Can we at least talk about it?"

Dion looked at Booker and inclined his head. Booker put in his earbuds, turned, and faced the window.

Imani sat on his bed, her hands in her lap. Dion sighed aggressively and racked his hand over his head.

"Say what you got to say," he barked.

Imani stiffened.

"I feel like you aren't saying everything you feel. Like you won't talk to me."

Dion closed his eyes and took a deep breath. Remembering all that gas lighting talk Lanelle kept bugging him with. *Honesty,* he thought.

"I'm trying my best," he said in a low whisper.

"But you said you forgave me," Imani shrieked.

Dion clenched his fist and when he relaxed his hand, He took another deep breath, still not turning around.

"I did forgive you, and I stayed with you. I am working on the trust thing."

"You don't trust me?" Imani asked in a small voice.

"No. All I can think about is whether there's a bug in my bag—or who else you might be telling my business to."

Imani scowled and shifted her weight. "Well if that's the case then why are we together?" she asked.

Dion turned around to finally face her as he put his hand behind his back. Booker felt the temperature drop and turned over his shoulder, peeking at Dion. The look on his face made him text Lanelle.

Booker: 911 Dion and Imani arguing and it's getting cold

"I don't care nothing about your ultimatums Imani,"

She pouted and crossed her arms. "It's not an ultimatum. But," she sighed in frustration. "I don't know what to do here, Dion."

"Either give me time or you don't have to be here," he said pointedly.

"I'm here because I want to be here," she said. "And you talk about ultimatums."

There was an aggressive knock at the door and then it opened.

"Hey, Dion - oh hey Imani. I didn't know you were here. Dion where is your phone, can you come up? I am on Video Call with Mom and Dad."

Dion looked at Imani and turned towards Lanelle. "Alright let's go," he said without saying goodbye and walked out of the room.

As they got to the staircase leading to the girl's wing, Lanelle grabbed his arm and led him toward the door. "Where are we going?" he asked.

"To let off some steam," she replied.

* * *

Dion adjusted the wraps around his hands, rolling his shoulders as he bounced on the balls of his feet. Restlessness burned through him, his energy barely in check. The fight with Imani had left him raw, his emotions simmering beneath the surface, waiting for an excuse to explode. Lanelle was here to help, but he wasn't sure if he could keep himself from going too hard.

"You good?" she asked, shifting her stance.

Dion exhaled sharply through his nose. "Yeah. Just need to hit something."

Lanelle smirked and cracked her knuckles. "That's what I'm here for."

Silently she lunged, throwing a quick jab at his side. He sidestepped easily, pivoting on his heel as he countered with a smooth strike aimed at her ribs. She blocked it, the impact rattling through her forearm. He wasn't holding back much.

They circled each other, exchanging blows. The only sounds in the gym were the dull thuds of fists meeting flesh, the scuff of sneakers on the mat, and their heavy breathing. He was fast, but Lanelle had fought him enough times to anticipate his moves. She dodged a hook, ducking under his arm to deliver a sharp uppercut to his stomach. He grunted but didn't falter, grabbing her wrist and twisting, forcing her into a spin.

She twisted, using the momentum to break free, and came at him again. This time, she faked right before snapping a kick at his side. He blocked, barely, frustration tightening his expression.

"Come on," she taunted. "I know you can do better."

A growl rumbled in Dion's throat. His next strike was harder, faster. She barely managed to block it before he came at her again, his movements becoming sharper, more erratic. His breathing turned heavy, muscles coiled with tension—

He felt a slip. His fist glowed faintly just before impact, and though he pulled back at the last second, the force sent Lanelle stumbling back. The gym's overhead lights flickered. The air between them chilled, mist curling from his fingertips where frost had begun to form.

"Dion," she warned, shaking off the tingling in her arms. "We said no magic."

His jaw tightened, hands clenching into fists at his sides. The cold emanating from his skin was undeniable now, sharp as a winter wind. "I'm trying."

She studied him, chest rising and falling with each breath. He was unraveling. "You don't have to hold it all in, you know."

He let out a harsh laugh. "Yeah? And what, let it loose on you?"

"I can handle it," Lanelle squared her shoulders. "You're frustrated. Use it. Just control it."

His eyes darkened, conflict warring inside them. Then, finally, he exhaled, tension easing slightly. "Fine."

A shimmer of frost flickered at his fingertips, brief and contained, before he lunged at her again.

Dion's speed doubled as he struck, forcing her onto the defensive. He was relentless, his sharp, calculated blows pushing her back. She ducked under a high kick, rolling to the side just as his fist slammed into the space she'd just vacated, a thin layer of ice crackling over the mat.

Lanelle retaliated with a flurry of punches, aiming for his ribs, his stomach, his jaw. He blocked most of them, but one slipped past his guard, snapping his head to the side. Instead of stepping back, he surged forward, spinning low and sweeping her legs out from under her. She hit the mat hard but rolled with it, pushing off her hands to spring back up just as he charged again.

They clashed in the center, exchanging rapid strikes—punches, kicks, feints, and counters. Sweat dripped down Dion's temples, steam rising faintly from his skin as his cold magic met the warm gym air. Lanelle's eyes burned with determination, pushing herself to match his pace.

She ducked beneath his next punch and, using his momentum against him, grabbed his arm and flipped him over her shoulder. He hit the mat with a thud, but before she could press her advantage, he rolled to his feet, his breath curling in a visible mist as the temperature around him dropped.

Lanelle wiped her mouth and grinned. "Come on, Dion. Let's see what you've really got."

His lips curled into a smirk. "You asked for it."

With a surge of energy, he lunged at her, this time with his magic fully unleashed, ice spreading beneath his feet as he closed the distance.

Dion thrust his hand forward, shards of ice forming in midair which pelted toward Lanelle in rapid succession. She reacted instantly, summoning a wall of fire that melted the first wave before rolling to the side to avoid the next. Flames flickered along her arms as she countered, sending a jet of heat his way.

The air sizzled where ice met fire, steam rising between them. Dion narrowed his eyes, dodging as best he could while sending another volley of icicles toward her. Lanelle countered each one, her flames spiraling in controlled bursts, meeting his cold energy in crackling bursts of vapor.

He pushed forward, freezing the ground beneath her feet, forcing her to adjust her footing. She ignited the air around her, melting the frost before launching a concentrated fireball straight at him. He dodged, just barely, feeling the heat graze past him.

They clashed again, ice and fire colliding in a battle of sheer will. But as the steam swirled between them, Lanelle's expression shifted. She broke away with a frustrated huff.

"Dion, we agreed—no magic," she snapped, her flames flickering out. Her fists remained clenched at her sides, but her stance was less battle-ready, more wary.

Dion's breath came fast, the cold mist still curling off his fingertips. He wanted to argue, to tell her he couldn't help it, but the words stuck in his throat.

Lanelle exhaled sharply, crossing her arms. "You're still mad at Imani, tell me what happened."

Dion clenched his jaw, ice cracking beneath his feet as he forced himself to stillness. "I don't want to talk about it."

She huffed, her fiery glow dimming. "Then maybe you should before you burn—or freeze—yourself out."

Dion sighed, rolling his shoulders as he stepped back into his stance. Lanelle watched him for a moment, then nodded, taking her own stance once more.

"Alright," she said, her voice softer but still firm. "No magic this time. Just you and me."

Dion nodded, his tension easing just slightly. "Fine."

Without another word, they moved, fists meeting in a familiar rhythm, the heat of their emotions giving way to the simplicity of the fight.

The Garden Said 'No'

Damien twisted the bracelet on his wrist. As the air shimmered with magic, he grabbed Ayana's hand, pulling them both through the portal back to The Garden. The air was thick with an eerie stillness. Everything had changed. The last time they were here, they had to look off in the distance to see where The Garden was starting to die. Now, it was closer.

The once vibrant foliage was muted, the life of the place still draining away like sand slipping through an hourglass.

Ayana crossed her arms. "Feels even worse today."

Damien exhaled, rolling his shoulders. "Then we don't have time to waste."

They stepped forward. The vines trembled as they passed, the trees whispering.

Their path from yesterday still bore signs of their struggle—the disturbed dirt where they had scrambled away from the serpent, the snapped vines of their makeshift trap. But the stone pedestal remained, its runes glowing faintly like it was waiting for them.

Ayana reached out, running her fingers over the strange symbols. "Alright, where were we? *'Only when shadows dance and truth is lost will the heart be revealed.'*" She shook her head.

"I hate riddles."

Damien crouched, scanning the area around the pedestal. "Shadows dance...what if it means literal shadows?"

Ayana squinted at the trees. "Like at a certain time of day?"

"Maybe." Damien studied the clearing. The sun had shifted since yesterday, casting new shadows across the ground. His eyes followed the way the branches created dark patterns over the pedestal's stone surface.

Ayana glanced up, watching the light filter through the leaves. "If we need shadows to move, we might have to wait until—"

A deep groan rumbled through the air, cutting her off.

Damien shot to his feet. "What was that?"

Ayana turned, her eyes scanning the tree line. "That wasn't the snake, was it?"

The air shifted, heavy and oppressive. Then the ground shook.

A low, guttural growl echoed through the trees. Not the serpent—but something else.

Damien's expression darkened. "We need to move. Now."

Ayana took a step back as the shadows beneath the trees began to shift unnaturally. Darkness pooled and stretched, coiling like living tendrils.

A pair of glowing yellow eyes.

Ayana's breath caught in her throat. "No. Nope. Absolutely not."

A hulking figure materialized from the darkness—its form wolf-like, but unnaturally tall, with elongated limbs and jagged, shifting fur that seemed to blur at the edges. Its eyes locked onto them with a hunger that sent chills racing down Ayana's spine.

Damien grabbed her wrist. "Run!"

They bolted just as the creature lunged. It moved faster than it should have, gliding, a living shadow bleeding through reality. Ayana felt the rush of air as it nearly swiped her back.

"Where are we even running?" she gasped.

Damien gritted his teeth. "Anywhere but here!"

They burst back into the main path, but the creature was relentless. It didn't seem deterred by the daylight creeping through the trees. If anything, it thrived in the half-light of the cursed garden.

Then, as suddenly as the chase had begun, a powerful voice echoed through the clearing.

"Enough."

The beast halted, its yellow eyes snapping toward the source.

Ayana skidded to a stop, panting. Damien followed suit, his hand tightening around his knife.

From between two massive, gnarled trees, a figure emerged—tall, cloaked in deep blue robes embroidered with silver thread. A hood shadowed their face, but their presence radiated authority.

The creature let out a low snarl, but did not advance.

The figure lifted a single hand. "You are not yet ready to see the core." Their voice was smooth, almost ageless. "Leave, or be consumed by what lurks here."

Ayana took a step forward. "Who are you? What do you mean we're not ready?"

The figure tilted their head slightly, but did not answer. Instead, they turned their gaze toward the dark beast, and with a flick of their hand, the creature dissolved into swirling mist.

Damien's pulse pounded in his ears. "What the hell is going on?"

The cloaked figure turned to them. "You have come too soon.

The path is not yet open."

Ayana clenched her fists. "So what, we just leave? Again?"

Silence.

Then, the ground beneath them trembled once more. This time, The Garden itself seemed to reject them. The trees swayed unnaturally, the air thickened like a vice around their lungs, and the sky darkened as if a storm were forming out of nowhere.

Damien grabbed Ayana's arm. "We don't have a choice!"

The pressure around them grew unbearable. They turned and sprinted back toward the entrance. The world blurred around them, shadows clawing at the edges of their vision. It felt as though The Garden itself was forcing them out.

Then—just as suddenly as it began—the pressure lifted.

They stumbled forward, past the threshold, and into open air. The sky above was clear once more. The Garden stood behind them, its colors dull, its entrance still and lifeless.

Ayana hunched over, catching her breath.

Damien exhaled sharply. "Next time we need to figure out what the hell it means by 'ready.'"

But the Gym Says YASS

Back on campus, Ayana sprinted across the quad, late for practice. She hated that when they are in The Garden, they lose time but she needed to go with Damien to save Michael.

As she approached the gym she heard music bumping and basketball all at the same time.

She burst through the door and saw the team on one half of the court doing their stretches. She rushed over and dropped her things, falling into the stretches with everyone else. Jade lifted her head up from the front row and peered at her.

Ayana mouthed sorry, her cheeks heating.

It was noisy in the gym. The boys were practicing on the other side of the court and it was an absolute mess.

The boys were supposed to be practicing drills, but instead, they were showing off—and failing spectacularly.

Booker launched a half-court shot that bricked off the rim so hard it bounced out of bounds. Dion went for a behind-the-back pass that sailed straight into the bleachers. Quashaw tried to dunk but miscalculated, missing the rim entirely and landing hard on his feet. Damien was too busy smirking at Ayana to realize the ball had even been passed to him. It smacked him square in the chest before rolling to the sidelines.

A sharp whistle cut through the air.

"Are y'all *trying* to embarrass me?" Coach bellowed, storming onto the court. His clipboard smacked against his thigh with every step. "Because right now, you're out here lookin' like a comedy show instead of a basketball team!"

Ayana smirked, exchanging glances with Tariana. This was way more entertaining than their routine.

"We're just getting loose, Coach," Dion said, spinning the ball on his finger like he hadn't just gotten clocked by it.

"Loose?" Coach echoed, eyes bulging. "You better tighten up before I have y'all running suicides till next week!"

Dion snuck another glance at the dance team. Quashaw nudged him with his elbow, grinning.

Coach saw it. "Oh, so that's what this is?" His voice rose, and the boys instantly looked serious. "You wanna impress somebody? How 'bout you impress me by making a free throw, huh? Or maybe just—*I don't know*—CATCHING THE BALL?!"

Ayana snorted, biting her lip to keep from laughing.

"Run it again!" Coach barked. "And if one more of you clowns tries some flashy, no-look pass that don't connect, *all* y'all are running till the gym closes!"

Damien groaned but grabbed the ball. "Alright, alright, we got it."

Quashaw smirked. "So, uh...no dunk contest?"

Coach's glare could've set the court on fire. "LINE UP," he roared.

All the boys groaned.

Ayana shook her head, watching as the boys scrambled back into position.

The steady rhythm of the music pulsed through the gym as Ayana and Tariana moved in sync with the rest of the dance team. Ayana lost herself in the beat. Every movement was sharp, fluid—her footwork crisp, her arms precise.

Tariana danced beside her, equally locked in, moving like the music had been made just for them. The rest of the team matched their energy, but Ayana felt it—she was *on* today.

On the other side of the gym, Coach had been running drills with the basketball team, but his booming voice had gone quiet. He'd stopped, arms crossed, watching.

As the song ended, the team hit their final pose. Ayana straightened, wiping sweat from her brow.

"Damn, girl," Tariana said, breathing hard. "You ate that up."

Before Ayana could respond, Coach's voice cut through the gym.

"AYANA!"

She turned, slightly startled.

Coach stepped onto their side of the court. "You always dance like that?"

Ayana blinked. "Um...yeah?"

Coach glanced at Jade, who was sipping from her water bottle. "Why is she back there?" he asked, jerking his chin toward Ayana's usual spot in the middle rows.

Jade lifted a brow. "I mean...she's good, but—"

"She's better than good," Coach cut in. "That girl just outdanced half this team and y'all got her in the back? Move her up front. Put her next to you."

A few dancers exchanged glances. Jade hesitated for half a second. "Alright. Ayana, take the front row with me."

Ayana's heart jumped. *Front row? Next to Jade?*

She tried to keep her cool, but Tariana elbowed her, whispering, "Told you, you killed it."

Ayana stepped forward, swallowing the nerves bubbling in her chest. This was big.

Coach clapped his hands once. "Alright, let's see it again. Make it count."

The music kicked in, and this time, Ayana was front and center. She wasn't about to waste the opportunity. Her body moved instinctively, each motion fueled by the same intensity she had in the back. She hit every move with precision, her rhythm locked in—but then, the music cut off abruptly.

"Hold on, hold on." Coach's voice rang out, sharp and expectant.

Ayana's breath came in quick pants as she turned to face him.

"Ayana, where is all that energy I saw in the back?"

Her heart thudded. "What am I doing wrong?" she asked, frustration creeping in.

"You're not doing anything wrong," Coach said, pacing. "But you're holding back. You had fire before, but now? Now, you're just executing the moves. I don't want precision—I want presence. Give me what you had in the back."

Ayana blinked. She thought she was dancing the same way. Had she really dulled herself down?

Coach studied the group, then pointed. "Alright, new formation. Jade, Tariana, and Ayana, front and center. Triangle setup. Jade, you're the inverted point. The rest of you, staggered behind in a zig-zag."

The dancers shifted positions.

Coach clapped once. "Let's go again! Five, six, seven, eight—"

The beat dropped, and this time, they *attacked* the routine. Tariana shot Ayana a quick wink before they plunged into movement, bodies hitting each beat with sharpness and flair.

Energy rippled between them, feeding off each other's styles, blending technique with raw intensity.

Coach clapped, her voice rising over the music. "YES! Yes, that's it!"

They slammed into their final pose, holding it steady before letting go, chests heaving, sweat glistening under the lights.

Coach nodded approvingly, arms crossed. "Now I *see* it."

Ayana wiped her forehead, still catching her breath. "See what, Coach?"

Coach smirked but addressed the team.

"The talent show is tomorrow, and our first game is Saturday morning. Regular practice is still on, but because of the show, we're pushing it to 8:30."

Groans echoed through the gym.

Coach rolled her eyes. "Yeah, yeah, I hear you. Suck it up. I want everyone in the auditorium at *six p.m. sharp* tomorrow. Come *dressed* and *prepped.*"

With that, he dismissed them.

As they made their way toward the locker room, Ayana frowned. "Prepped? What does that mean?"

Tariana slung an arm around her. "It means we have to have our makeup done for the show and all the game."

Ayana's stomach bottomed out. "I don't wear makeup."

Jade appeared beside them, smirking. "I can help with that."

"And Lanelle's good at it too," Tariana added.

Jade held up a hand. "Correction—I can't *apply* it for you. I suck at that. But I *can* help you shop for it."

Ayana smiled, relieved. "Thanks."

"Then Lanelle's got the application part," Tariana said.

Jade stretched, rolling her shoulders. "We can hit the store after we shower and change."

Ayana hesitated. "Wait...how are we getting there? I thought we weren't allowed to leave campus."

Jade smirked. "First and second-years can't." She spun on her heel, heading for the showers. Before disappearing inside, she tossed a glance over her shoulder.

"By the way," she called, feigning nonchalance. "Y'all did good or whatever."

Ayana shot a text off to her Mom. *On the dance team, need makeup for games. Money please?*

Blending, Bleeding, and Besties

Ayana, Lanelle, and Jade trudged back from the store, their arms weighed down with bags filled with makeup, brushes, and other last-minute essentials. Ayana had spent every penny her mom had given her, and when she came up short, Jade quietly covered a few extras, insisting they were "must-haves."

Back in the dorm, Lanelle unlocked the door and swung it open, immediately grabbing one of Ayana's bags, and dumping its contents onto the bed.

"Alright," she said, clapping her hands together. "Let's see what we're working with."

Jade took one look at the explosion of beauty products and held up her hands. "And *this* is where I take my exit," she announced, already backing toward the door. "Y'all have fun."

"Thanks. Really," Ayana said, meeting her gaze with quiet gratitude.

Jade just smirked.

As soon as the door shut, Lanelle turned back to Ayana, rolling up her sleeves like she was preparing for a serious operation. "Okay, the best way to do this is for us to do it together. That way, you'll actually *learn* how to do it yourself next time."

Ayana noticed Lanelle's desk had been transformed into a full-fledged beauty station, complete with a mirror ringed with bright bulbs.

"I wasn't sure if you got the tools or just the makeup," Lanelle admitted, tilting her head. "But lucky for you, I had an extra mirror, some wipes, and this pack of brushes Dion got me." She smirked. "Only time I use 'em is when I forget to wash my regular ones."

She nudged the brushes toward Ayana. "You can have these. Guess I'll just have to start washing mine like I'm *supposed* to."

"Thanks," Ayana said, touched by the gesture. She rummaged through the bags. "We got sponges, but that's about it. I'm gonna run to the bathroom real quick, then we can get started. My stomach's been hurting all day."

Lanelle arched a brow. "Listen, do *not* go blowing up my bathroom." She started organizing the makeup into neat categories.

Tariana, lounging on the bed, cackled. "Girl, if you gotta go, you gotta go," she shrugged.

Ayana rolled her eyes and disappeared into the bathroom. A few seconds later, a sharp, panicked shriek rang out.

"Umm, guys? I need help."

Tariana wrinkled her nose. "Yeah, no. Whatever it is, I *am not* helping you do *anything* in the bathroom."

Lanelle called out at the same time, "What's wrong?"

The door cracked open slightly, and Ayana peeked out, looking horrified. "I think I just got my period. This is bad. We have a performance tomorrow."

Tariana sucked her teeth. "*That's* what you're freaking out about? Girl, just wear a tampon."

Lanelle gave Tariana a pointed look before turning back to

Ayana. "Wait...you *just* got it? Like, for the first time?"

Ayana nodded hesitantly.

Lanelle exhaled dramatically, shaking her head. "Damn. Alright, hold up." She shot Tariana a look. "Go grab the emergency stash."

Tariana groaned but rolled off the bed, muttering under her breath as she dug through her drawer.

"Don't worry, girl," Lanelle assured Ayana. "We got you."

Tariana's head snapped up. "Oh, girl, no need for all that. *SelfVideo to the rescue!*" She grabbed her phone, pulled up a tutorial video, and slid it—along with the emergency stash—carefully under the bathroom door, turning her head like she was handling a hostage negotiation.

"There. Watch, learn, and handle your business."

Lanelle snorted, shaking her head. "Welcome to womanhood, Ayana."

A dramatic groan echoed from behind the door, making the girls laugh.

Ten minutes later, Ayana finally emerged from the bathroom.

"*Dang,* about time," Tariana groaned, flopping back on the bed dramatically. "I was about to send a search party."

Lanelle shot her a look before turning her attention to Ayana. Her expression softened. "You good?"

Ayana hesitated, her cheeks warming. "Yeah, I guess. My stomach still hurts, though."

Tariana sat up, eyeing her curiously. "Do you...*feel* anything?"

Ayana stood there for a second, listening to her body like she was waiting for something awful to happen. After a beat, she shook her head. "No...not really."

Lanelle nodded, satisfied. "Good. There's painkillers in the bag—take one, and let's get this show on the road."

Ayana exhaled, relieved, as she grabbed the bottle and popped open the cap. She wasn't sure what she'd been expecting—discomfort, awkwardness, *a literal disaster*—but so far, she was surviving.

"Alright, now that *that's* handled," Lanelle said, rubbing her hands together. "It's time to make you look *performance-ready.*"

Tariana grinned. "Translation: We're about to turn you into a *baddie.*"

Ayana groaned playfully. "Y'all are doing a *lot* right now."

Lanelle smirked. "Girl, you have *no* idea."

Lanelle sat next to Ayana, telling her which products to grab, showing her what tools to use, and how to apply the products. When they were finished, Lanelle and Ayana had full glam makeup looks.

Tariana clapped her hands. "YES," she exclaimed. You look good girl. we about to kill it tomorrow. I'm going to have to step my game up to compete."

Ayana's cheeks heated as she caught her reflection in the mirror. The transformation was *real.*

"Girl, *please,*" she scoffed, tilting her head and checking herself out from different angles. The foundation was smooth, her eyes popped with just the right amount of shimmer, and her lips—glossy but not overdone—gave her a fresh, effortless glow.

She grabbed her phone, snapped a selfie, and sent it to her mom and little sister with a quick, *Who even is this?!*

Tariana peered over her shoulder, smirking. "Ohhh, we're feeling ourselves now, huh?"

Ayana rolled her eyes but couldn't hide her smile. "I mean...I don't look half bad."

Lanelle snorted. "Half bad? Girl, you look *fire.* If you don't step out tomorrow with this same energy, I swear—"

A ping from Ayana's phone cut her off. She glanced down at the screen.

Mom: *My baby is all grown up! You look beautiful, sweetie. Hope you're feeling okay.*

Ryan: *OMG!! WHOA. YOU LOOK SO PRETTY! Can you do mine like that next time?!*

Ayana laughed, shaking her head. "Ryan is so dramatic."

Tariana grinned. "She's got a point, though."

Ayana set her phone down, her nerves settling. Maybe this whole thing wasn't so bad after all.

We Came, We Saw, We Sweated

Lanelle pushed open the heavy double doors of the auditorium, the scent of stage dust and faintly burnt popcorn from the lobby concession stand greeted her. The place was already alive with movement, an electric energy buzzing through the air as performers stretched, tuned instruments, and ran through last-minute rehearsals.

She stepped inside, her heels echoing against the polished floor. She'd dressed for the occasion—high-waisted jeans that hugged her figure just right, a cute fitted top in a deep emerald green that flattered her skin tone, and matching heels that gave her a little extra height. Her makeup was flawless, of course—soft but striking, with a sharp winged liner and a subtle highlight catching the dim stage lights.

She'd coordinated her colors without even meaning to—only realizing *after* she'd left her dorm that Booker had on a shirt in almost the exact same shade of green. Not that she minded.

It wasn't like they planned it, but the thought of them unintentionally matching had her smirking—until the smirk faded into something closer to unease. Lately, she'd been hanging out with him and Jalen a *lot*, and there were moments— quick glances, small smiles, inside jokes—that felt...good. Especially with Booker.

But then there was Jalen.

Her stomach twisted again. *Damn.*

She liked Jalen. He was sweet, steady. He looked at her like she was something special, and she *should* like that. She *did* like that. But part of her wondered if she was leading him on, stringing him along when her head—*and her heart*—felt pulled in too many directions.

And now, here she was, matching with Booker like they had coordinated outfits, something that would no doubt get people talking.

She exhaled sharply and shook her head. *Focus, Lanelle. You're here to perform, not spiral.*

The dim stage lights, cast long, dramatic shadows across the polished wood floor, but a few spotlights flickered as tech crew members adjusted their angles. Shuffling feet echoed as the dance team worked through a light practice, their movements sharp even in half-energy mode.

Lanelle paused near the entrance, watching Ayana, Tariana, and the rest of the squad mark through their steps. Ayana was already in the zone, her body moving with the rhythm even as she held back from going full out. Tariana whispered to her, and they both snickered before snapping back into formation, their sneakers squeaking against the stage as they hit their cues.

Beyond them, a girl with a violin tuned her instrument in the far corner, adjusting her bow with meticulous care. On the opposite side, a trio of singers harmonized quietly, their voices blending so seamlessly that Lanelle got chills, despite herself.

Backstage, students rushed to set up props and check costumes. Someone was wrestling with a stubborn microphone stand, grumbling under their breath, while another student tested the stage curtain, peeking through to get a glimpse of the slowly filling audience.

Lanelle smirked, shaking her head. *Controlled chaos. Exactly how these things always go.*

She made her way toward the dancers, rolling her shoulders as she prepared to warm up. "Y'all looking decent or whatever," she teased, earning an exaggerated eye roll from Tariana.

"We *are* decent," Tariana shot back. "But after this, we'll be unstoppable."

Ayana, adjusting her stance, gave Lanelle a smirk. "You ready?"

Lanelle stretched out her arms, feeling the familiar excitement build. "Always."

At exactly seven o'clock Dean Barkner got in the stage and introduced the MC and the show began.

A few acts went on before Lanelle and Booker. Sitting in the front row with the rest of the people, she was clapping and bobbing along with all of the acts.

"They killing it tonight," Booker said, leaning over to her.

"Yes, makes me a little nervous. The dance team is good to. I hope we win."

"Just breath, in and out," he said.

"Our song is solid and people will love that it's original and not us covering a song like the other singing acts."

Of course, she thought. *we have an edge.*

Booker squeezed her shoulder. "Relax Nell we got this."

Lanelle took a deep breath and let it out slowly. Then her phone pinged.

Tariana: *IT'S SHOWTIME, BABY!!!* 🎤🔥🎵

Ayana: *Lanelle, you ready? We KNOW you about to kill it.*

Booker: *No doubt. You 'bout to shut it DOWN.* 🎧🎤

Dion: *Pfft, shut it down? She's about to make history.* ▨

Lanelle: *Okay, but what if I forget the lyrics? What if I freeze? What if I just...combust?* ✎

Quashawn: *Then we will collectively act like it was part of the performance. No one will ever know.*

Damien: *Or I'll cause a "technical difficulty" and cut the lights so you can recover.*

Tariana: *I swear, y'all are NOT helping.*

Dion: *Okay but fr, Lanelle, you've been KILLING rehearsals. Ain't no way you messing up tonight.*

Ayana: *Facts. Just breathe, lock in, and let that voice do what it does.*

Quashawn: *And don't let Booker drown you out with his extra sound effects.* 👀

Booker: *Why am I catching strays?*

Damien: *Because we know you.* 🎤

Tariana: *Lanelle, just zone in. You were made for this.*

Lanelle: *Y'all are making me emotional before I even get on stage. STOP.* 🖤

Dion: *Nah, we hyping you up 'cause you DESERVE it. Now go EAT.* 🍽️🔥

Booker: *And trust me, I got you on the mix. We about to make magic.* 🎧✨

Quashawn: *And if you start feeling yourself too much, I'll remind you you're still one of us.* 😁

Ayana: *LMAOOO*

Lanelle: *I hate y'all. But I love y'all. Let's do this.* 🪄✨

Lanelle stood just offstage, heart hammering, fingers curled tightly around the microphone. The heavy velvet curtain shielded her from the audience, but she could *feel* them—rows of students, teachers, and parents. The auditorium was packed, the lights casting a warm golden glow over the eager faces waiting to be entertained.

Beside her, Booker adjusted his headphones around his neck, fingers flying over the DJ board as he double-checked the sound levels. He shot her a confident smirk. "You ready?"

Lanelle let out a slow breath. "I think so."

Booker chuckled. "Nah, you *know* so." He bumped her shoulder. "Let's go show 'em."

The announcer's voice boomed through the speakers. "Next up, Lanelle and Booker bringing us something special—give it up for them!"

The crowd erupted into applause and cheers as the curtain pulled back.

The stage lights hit her all at once, bathing everything in a golden haze. Lanelle forced herself to move, her heels clicking against the glossy stage floor as she stepped forward. She held the mic close, fingers steady despite the nerves prickling under her skin.

Behind her, Booker took his spot at the DJ booth, one hand on the turntable, the other adjusting knobs as the intro beat hummed through the speakers, deep and rich.

In the audience, she spotted her friends immediately. Tariana was the loudest—hands cupped around her mouth as she screamed, *"LET'S GOOOOO!"* so loud that a few heads turned. Ayana clapped hard, eyes wide with excitement, nodding like she *knew* Lanelle was about to deliver. Dion, Damien, and Quashawn stood up, hyping her up before the first note even dropped. "That's my girl!!" Dion shouted, pointing dramatically. Even from the stage, she could see Quashawn recording on his phone, probably already crafting a ridiculous caption for his story.

Lanelle smiled, their energy seeping into her, grounding her.

Then—the beat dropped.

Booker worked the turntables, effortlessly blending the music, the deep bass rolling through the auditorium. The track pulsed beneath her, steady and strong, and she took a breath—then let it all go.

The first note left her lips, smooth and rich, floating over the beat like she was *meant* to be here.

The crowd responded instantly. A wave of cheers and claps filled the space, heads bobbing to the rhythm. Someone in the back held up their phone flashlight, and within seconds, others followed—tiny white lights swaying in the darkness.

She *felt* it now.

The nerves melted away, replaced by something electric. She closed her eyes for a moment, lost in the music, in the way her voice intertwined with the melody.

Booker, in sync with her every move, hyped up the crowd between transitions, his voice sliding in seamlessly. "*Y'all hear that?!*" he called, throwing a hand in the air. "*Make some noise for Lanelle!*"

The crowd *roared.*

Lanelle grinned, stepping into the moment fully, letting her voice soar.

This was it.

This was *her* moment.

And she was owning every second of it.

As Lanelle hit the last note, the beat faded, leaving only the echoes of applause crashing through the auditorium. She let the sound wash over her, chest heaving, a wide smile spreading across her face.

Booker pointed at her from behind the DJ booth, grinning.

"*That's how you do it!*"

She blew a playful kiss to the crowd before slipping offstage, heart still racing. Ayana and Tariana met her the second she stepped behind the curtain, bouncing with excitement.

"*You ate that!*" Ayana gushed.

"I mean, we knew you'd kill it, but *DAMN* girl!" Tariana added, squeezing her in a quick hug.

Lanelle barely had time to catch her breath before the next announcement rang out:

"And now, give it up for your school's dance team!**"**

The crowd erupted once more as the lights dimmed. The stage was now *theirs.*

A single bassline hummed through the speakers, low and ominous. The dancers stood poised in formation—heads bowed, bodies tense, the calm before the storm.

Booker, still behind the booth, nodded in approval. He spun a dial, and the bass dropped hard.

BOOM.

Ayana and Tariana *snapped* into motion.

The team's movements were crisp, their bodies slicing through the air with sharp precision. Tariana was in her element, all swagger and style, hitting each move with a confidence that made it look effortless. Ayana, smooth and controlled, balanced Tariana's boldness with graceful power. Their chemistry onstage was undeniable—the push and pull of two dancers who *knew* how to feed off each other's energy.

The crowd *felt* it.

Damien sat on the edge of his seat, eyes locked onto Ayana. He was completely *lost* in her performance.

His girl was *glowing.*

He had always known Ayana was good, but tonight? She was

something *else.* The way she moved, the way she *owned* the stage—it was mesmerizing. He could feel the pride swelling in his chest, his hands instinctively clapping along with the beat.

Dion nudged him with a grin. "Bruh, your girl is showing *out* tonight."

Damien just shook his head, a slow smile creeping across his lips. "She's killin' it."

Meanwhile, Quashawn was *yelling.* "*YOOOO! THEY DID NOT COME TO PLAY TONIGHT and THAT'S MY SISTER!!*" His phone was *locked in* on Tariana and Ayana as they led the squad through their routine.

The formation shifted, and the energy *exploded* as the breakdown hit. The spotlight hit *just* the three of them.

Ayana twirled, landing perfectly into a sharp isolation, her gaze locking with Tariana's. Tariana smirked, responding with a smooth roll of her shoulders before hitting a fierce stomp that sent shockwaves through the floor.

Jade fed off their energy, stepping forward into her own moment—a powerful spin into a full drop, landing effortlessly before popping back up into place.

The crowd *lost it.*

Damien was out of his seat now, clapping and whistling.

Tariana, feeling the energy, amped it up even more. She hit the final beat *hard*, throwing an arm around Ayana as they struck their last pose, with Jade crouched low between them, arms spread wide like they had just *conquered* the stage.

And then—silence.

A beat of stillness.

Then the auditorium *erupted.*

Whistles. Cheers. Feet stomping against the floor.

Ayana, Tariana, and Jade, breathless but grinning, stood

frozen for a second, soaking it all in.

Tariana turned to them, eyes wide with excitement. "Oh yeah. We just ATE that."

Jade flicked her hair over her shoulder, smirking. "Obviously."

Ayana laughed, chest still rising and falling. "Completely."

From the audience, Damien just shook his head in awe, clapping harder than anyone.

"And the winner is," the announcer began. Pausing for dramatic effect.

"For most creative TIFF AND THE DANCERETTES," The crowd cheered as Tiff went up to get the trophy.

"And now for crowd favorite," The announcer continued his pause for anticipation build up routine. "THE DOUGLAS HIGH DANCE TEAM."

The moment the announcer declared them the crowd favorite, the entire auditorium *exploded* again. Cheers. Stomping feet. The thunderous energy of the audience felt like an earthquake rattling the walls.

Tariana and Ayana barely had time to catch their breath before Jade shot forward, bouncing on her heels as she made her way to collect their trophy. She snatched it with a victorious grin, holding it high above her head as the team cheered behind her.

From the DJ booth, Booker let out a low whistle, shaking his head in amusement. "Man, y'all really had the crowd in the *palm* of your hands."

The announcer laughed into the mic. "Our runners-up for crowd favorite are Lanelle and Booker! It was a *close* one, y'all. The crowd made it *real* hard to determine who they liked better."

Lanelle, still riding the high of her performance, let out a surprised laugh as she exchanged a glance with Booker.

"Ayyyeee," Dion called, making his way toward them. "Second place but *still* eating the whole competition up? That's a *win* in my book."

"Bro, don't act like you ain't just *body* the whole stage," Quashawn added, throwing an arm around Lanelle's shoulder. "You was up there giving *main character energy* the *entire* time."

Lanelle smirked, flicking her hair over her shoulder. "I *did* what needed to be done."

Booker leaned into the mic, voice smooth as always. "And let's not forget *who* was keeping the sound tight." He pointed to himself.

Damien laughed, shaking his head. "Oh, here he go."

"Boy, if you don't—" Tariana teased, rolling her eyes.

Lanelle playfully shoved Booker. "Okay, okay. You did your *job.* Let's not act like you invented DJing."

Before Booker could fire back, Ayana wiped the sweat off her forehead, still catching her breath from the performance. "Y'all... that was *insane.*" She turned to Damien, who had practically been hollering for her the whole time. "You good? You were out there like a whole *fan club.*"

Damien pulled her into a side hug, kissing the top of her head. "Good? *I'm great.* I mean, my girl just *shut it down.* Of course, I'm gonna act a fool."

Ayana blushed but playfully shoved him. "You *stay* acting a fool."

Lanelle spun the trophy in her hands, her grin never fading. "So, are we celebrating or what?"

Tariana groaned, stretching her arms overhead. "Man, I *wish.* But Coach wants another practice. *Tonight.*"

Lanelle's eyes widened. "What? *Tonight?*"

Ayana sighed. "Yup. She said since we're performing at the basketball game tomorrow, we need to be *flawless.*"

Damien made a face. "Did she *not* just see y'all eat up that stage?"

"Right?" Tariana scoffed. "But nah, apparently it's not enough."

Dion shook his head. "Coach be actin' like y'all going to the Olympics."

"*For real,*" Ayana muttered. "We barely cooled off, and now we gotta go sweat *again.*"

Quashawn smirked. "She's gonna run y'all so hard, you won't even remember winning *crowd favorite.*"

Tariana groaned but waved her hand dismissively. "It's fine. We'll just catch up with y'all later."

Lanelle shook her head. "Y'all *really* can't hang for five seconds?"

Ayana chuckled, "Practice starts at 8:30."

Booker stretched his arms over his head, yawning. "Welp. I guess that means the rest of us gotta celebrate *for* you."

"Uh, *duh,*" Dion said, as if it was the most obvious thing in the world.

Ayana shook her head, laughing as she and Tariana backed toward the hallway leading to the gym. "Y'all are *a mess.*"

Jade waved the trophy at them. "Y'all earned this, though. So go kill that practice."

Ayana and Tariana gave one last playful salute before heading off.

Lanelle exhaled, looking around at the group. "So...what *are* we doing?"

Quashawn grinned. "Something *fun.*"

Dion clapped his hands together. "Let's see what trouble we can get into."

Booker cracked his knuckles. "Now *that's* my kind of plan."

The night wasn't over just yet.

III

Brains, Bravery, and Barely Making It

Oh, So We're Just Out Here With Superpowers Now

Ayana stretched her arms behind her head, letting out a satisfied sigh as exhaustion settled into her bones. The talent show was over, practice was finally done, and the basketball game was tomorrow. After a long day of performing, running routines, and pushing through exhaustion, there was only one thing on her mind—bed.

She pulled out her phone and sent a quick text to Damien as she and Tariana made their way back toward the dorms.

Ayana: I am so ready to pass out.

Damien: Bet you won't even make it under the covers before you're out.

Ayana groaned dramatically. "I'm so ready for bed," she muttered, rubbing her face.

"One hundred percent," Tariana agreed, barely suppressing a yawn.

The quad was quiet aside from the soft rustle of trees in the evening breeze. The campus lights cast long shadows along the brick paths, the air cool against Ayana's skin. Just as they were about to round the corner toward the dorms, a voice cut through the night.

"Yo, T!"

They turned toward the sound of Quashawn's voice.

They spotted him near the pond, the usual crew sprawled out on the grass, laughing and talking. The energy was relaxed, a stark contrast to the chaos of earlier.

Tariana glanced at Ayana, eyebrows raised. "You tryna stop for a sec?"

Ayana hesitated. Sleep was calling her name, but seeing everyone chilling together, no stress, no pressure...it was tempting.

"Fine," she grumbled. "But only for a minute."

They made their way over, stepping onto the soft grass as Quashawn leaned back on his elbows, watching them

"What y'all doing?" Tariana asked, eyeing the half-eaten takeout containers beside him.

"We had dinner, now we're just chilling, waiting for y'all slow asses," Damien answered, holding out an arm toward Ayana.

She didn't hesitate—crossing the space and sinking onto his lap, his arms immediately wrapping around her waist. She leaned against him, the warmth of his embrace instantly grounding her.

"I hope y'all had fun," she mumbled, "but I'm going to bed. Coach was pushing hard today, and Jade was on edge."

Quashawn snorted. "She on edge or she just holding y'all accountable?"

Ayana sighed. "Both." She ran a hand through her hair. "She wasn't even wrong; she just wasn't taking anybody's excuses today."

Tariana nodded. "She was locked in. But that's kinda how she gets before performances."

"Yeah," Ayana admitted. "I get it, I do. Just wasn't in the

mood for all that tonight."

"Come on," Quashawn said, standing up. "I'll walk you to your dorm before you collapse on the sidewalk."

She stood, stretching once more before saying her goodbyes. Tariana gave her a lazy wave, already halfway into Booker's fries.

"Booker dipped early," Quashawn added as they started walking. "Jalen caught up with us after the show, and they ended up getting dinner together."

Ayana leaned in closer to Damien, lowering her voice as they watched Lanelle shift uncomfortably. "I'm guessing that was awkward."

"Hell yeah."

The answer didn't come from Damien.

It came from Dion—who was sitting a solid twenty feet away in the grass.

Ayana and Damien froze.

Their heads snapped toward Dion, who wasn't even looking at them, casually stretching his arms over his head like he didn't just defy the laws of physics.

Dion pushed himself up off the grass, dusting off his hoodie. "Anyway, I told Imani I'd meet up with her. I'm gonna dip." He turned to Lanelle. "You heading back too?"

Lanelle barely spared him a glance, still focused on Ayana and Damien's wide-eyed, horrified expressions.

She rolled her eyes. "Before y'all even start, nothing happened with Jalen. We were just chilling. Booker overreacted. There's nothing to tell."

She waited for a response.

None came.

Ayana and Damien were zeroed in on Dion.

Damien's expression hardened. "How did you hear what she said?"

Silence.

Dion and Lanelle exchanged a quick look—the kind of look that said way more than words ever could.

A look that confirmed everything.

Ayana's breath caught in her throat.

"...What was that?" she asked slowly, pointing between them.

Dion scratched the back of his head, looking suddenly very interested in the sky.

Lanelle sighed, rubbing her temples like she had been preparing for this moment. "I guess we're doing this now."

Damien leaned forward. "Doing what now?"

Lanelle didn't answer right away.

Instead, she took a long, measured breath. "Dion?"

Dion exhaled through his nose. "Yeah?"

"Go ahead."

Damien's eyebrows shot up. "WITH WHAT?!"

Dion let out a low groan, rolling his shoulders. "Alright. Cool. Guess we're doing this."

He met Ayana and Damien's stare head-on.

"I can hear things," he said simply. "And see through things. And freeze things."

Ayana's stomach dropped.

She wasn't sure what she was expecting him to say, but that wasn't it.

"...Excuse me?" Damien asked, voice wary.

Dion shifted his weight, stuffing his hands into his pockets. "I can hear things. From...far away."

Ayana's heartbeat picked up. "How far?"

Dion shrugged. "Depends. A lot of times, it's just background noise. But if I focus?" He tilted his head slightly, like he was tuning a radio station. "I can hear whole conversations from across a football field."

Silence.

Then—

"...I'm sorry. WHAT?!"

Damien staggered back like Dion just told him he could bend reality.

Ayana grabbed Damien's sleeve, her voice dead serious. "Damien. Do you understand what this means?"

His mouth opened, then closed.

Then opened again.

"Oh my god," he whispered, eyes darting between Dion and Lanelle. "HE'S HEARD EVERYTHING."

Dion smirked. "Yup."

Ayana let out a strangled noise. "I am never speaking freely again."

Damien dragged a hand down his face. "Bro. I—I have slandered so many people in your presence."

Dion grinned. "Oh yeah. You have."

Lanelle snorted. "Y'all are being dramatic."

Ayana whipped toward her. "and what about you? Do you have superpowers too?!"

Lanelle lifted a single eyebrow. "Obviously."

Damien swore under his breath. "Of course you do."

Ayana braced herself. "Okay. Hit me. What is it?"

Lanelle sipped her drink, unbothered. "I can see heat signatures. And control fire."

A beat of stunned silence.

Damien's jaw dropped. "You just got built-in thermal vision

and never thought to tell us?!"

Lanelle shrugged. "Y'all never asked."

Damien flopped onto the grass. "I need a minute."

Ayana exhaled. "I swear, this better not mean we're about to end up in some wild superhero plot."

Damien shot her a look. "We literally know about a magic garden."

A long pause.

Ayana blinked.

"...Oh, hell."

'So y'all yelling at us for holding out, but you just let slip a magic what now?!"

Dion raised an eyebrow, pulling out his phone and typing a quick message to Imani. **Running a little late. Something came up.**

He tucked his phone away and strolled over, dropping onto the grass beside Lanelle, his attention fully on Damien and Ayana. "Alright. Spill."

Damien dragged a hand down his face, inhaling deeply like he was about to tell them that Santa Claus was real and ran an underground fight club. "Okay...so, there's this garden—"

"A magic garden," Ayana corrected.

"Right." Damien exhaled. "A magic garden. We don't know exactly how it works, but it's—alive. It shifts. Moves. Feels things. And someone—" he paused, hesitating. "Someone's poisoned the core. We're trying to reach it, but we can never stay long enough to get far."

Lanelle and Dion exchanged a look, their previous disbelief shifting into something else.

Curiosity.

"How many people can you bring at one time?" Lanelle asked,

her tone sharp, calculated. "Can we help?"

Damien's head snapped up, surprise flickering across his face. "Y'all wanna help?"

Ayana spoke before he could. "Y'all would help?" she asked, hope creeping into her voice.

Lanelle scoffed, tilting her head with a smirk. "Duh. Fire would help out, right?"

Ayana blinked, then grinned.

"Hell yeah, it would."

* * *

Damien activated the bracelet, and the air around them shimmered, the barrier between their world and The Garden thinning until it pulled them through.

The shift was instantaneous.

The warm dusk light of their world was gone. Instead, the oppressive atmosphere of The Garden wrapped around them, thick and heavy.

Dion tensed immediately. He took in the atmosphere around him. "I thought ya'll said this was magical and pretty?" he asked.

The landscape had worsened overnight. What had once been dying slowly was now on the verge of collapse. The ground beneath them was cracked, webbed with dark veins that pulsed faintly. The air held a sickly stillness, the trees arching forward as if listening.

Ayana rubbed her arms. "It's worse."

Damien's gaze swept the area, taking in the twisted roots and dull, lifeless grass. "It's spreading faster than before."

Lanelle narrowed her eyes. Stepping toward a tree, she pressed a hand against the bark. The moment she made contact, heat radiated through her palm, images flashing behind her eyes. A golden glow. Twisting chains. A locked door.

She yanked her hand back. "Okay, yeah, there's some real bad energy running through this place."

Dion turned his head slightly, his enhanced hearing kicking in. "Something's moving."

Everyone stiffened.

Dion listened harder, filtering through the sounds—until he locked onto it. A deep, slow breathing. Not close, but watching.

"Not the wolf thing," he muttered. "Something else."

Ayana huffed. "Because of course there's something else."

Damien motioned for them to move. "Let's go. If we're gonna do this, we do it now."

They made their way toward the stone pedestal, stepping over the broken remnants of their last encounter. The runes were still there, glowing faintly, waiting.

Ayana ran her fingers over the symbols. "Last time, we didn't have time to figure this out before getting chased."

Dion glanced at the trees, still uneasy. "Yeah, let's avoid that part if we can."

Lanelle stepped beside Ayana, eyeing the stone. "That clue from last time—'*Only when shadows dance and truth is lost will the heart be revealed.*' That still makes zero sense."

Damien studied the way the sun cast its light across the clearing, the long shadows it formed against the stone. "Maybe it's about positioning. The way light and dark interact here."

Ayana frowned. "Except we can't control the sun."

Dion scoffed. "Yeah, unless one of y'all is secretly packing solar manipulation, I don't see how we—" He stopped mid-sentence, eyes snapping wide. "Wait."

Lanelle gave him a look. "What?"

Dion hesitated, then turned to Lanelle. "You control fire."

She blinked. "Yeah, we've established that."

"No, but—fire casts shadows."

A beat of silence.

Then realization clicked.

Ayana turned back to the pedestal. "Shadows dancing. It's not about the sun. It's about firelight."

Lanelle took a slow breath and lifted her hands, conjuring a small flame between her palms. The warm glow flickered against the stone, casting moving shadows across the runes.

"That is so cool," Ayana said staring.

Lanelle smirked and shrugged.

The air shifted.

The pedestal's glow intensified, the runes beginning to rearrange—sliding like puzzle pieces into place.

Lanelle's heartbeat kicked up. "It's working."

Damien stepped back as the ground beneath the pedestal shuddered, dust and dirt swirling as a hidden compartment began to open.

And then—

The deep, guttural growl returned. Dion went rigid. "Shit. We've got company."

The shadows between the trees coiled and moved, parting to reveal a familiar, terrifying sight—the wolf-like creature from before.

But this time, it wasn't alone. Another shape flickered beside it, something taller, more human but just as wrong. Its limbs were too long, its face obscured in darkness except for its piercing red eyes that gleamed like embers.

Ayana's stomach dropped. "Oh, hell no."

The wolf-creature let out a rattling snarl. The other creature raised a hand.

The shadows around them shifted unnaturally. Suddenly, the flames Lanelle had conjured flickered—then snuffed out.

Lanelle's breath hitched. "What the—"

The pedestal stopped moving.

The runes dimmed.

And the heavy force of The Garden itself bore down on them again.

Damien grabbed Ayana's wrist. "We need to get out. Now."

The Human like figure took a step forward, its voice like wind howling through a canyon.

"You are not welcome here."

Dion tensed. "Yeah? And you suck."

The shadows lashed outward, striking toward them like living whips.

Lanelle threw up a shield of fire. It flared bright—but the darkness swallowed it whole.

Ayana's breath caught. "We can't fight that."

Damien pulled her back as the wolf lunged. Dion barely shoved Lanelle aside before its claws tore through where she'd been standing.

The Garden trembled.

Lanelle hit the ground hard, rolling before she sprang back to her feet, eyes blazing. Her fire had never failed her before. The way the darkness had swallowed it, smothering it like it was nothing, sent a chill through her.

Dion yanked her arm, pulling her back just as the Human like creature swung its unnaturally long arm in their direction. The shadows stretched from its fingertips like tendrils, reaching for them.

"Nope, nope, nope—" Dion muttered as he shoved Lanelle aside and barely dodged the strike.

The wolf-like beast lunged at Ayana and Damien, its massive form moving with impossible speed. Damien barely had time to push Ayana out of the way before the beast's claws swiped through the air between them, missing by inches.

"We're not running this time!" Lanelle snapped, flames flaring from her palms again. "We have to take them down!"

Dion gritted his teeth. "Fine, but we need a better plan than hoping they burst into flames!"

The Human like creature turned its eerie, glowing eyes toward them and raised both arms. The air shifted—heavy and suffocating. The darkness on the ground rose up, curling into thick, clawed limbs.

Ayana scrambled to her feet, grabbed a rock and threw it. It hit, but passed right through the figure as if it were smoke.

"That was useless," she muttered.

Damien moved fast, slicing his knife through the air at the wolf creature's side. This time, it connected, but instead of cutting flesh, the blade rippled through its form like it was cutting through a thick mist.

The wolf snapped its head toward him, teeth glinting, and released a sound that wasn't a growl, but something deeper—a call.

A response came.

From the shadows, more figures began to emerge.

Lanelle swore under her breath. "Oh, that is not good."

Dion shot a glance at her. "Alright, screw subtlety—let's find out if your fire really doesn't work, or if we just weren't going hard enough."

He clapped his hands together and sent a shockwave of freezing air outward. The frost crawled over the wolf creature's legs, slowing it, making it snarl.

Lanelle took that moment to launch another fire blast—but this time, she focused on the frozen parts.

The flames hit.

And this time, they stuck.

The creature screeched, the ice crackling as the fire burned through instead of being smothered.

Lanelle's eyes lit up. "Okay, so we freeze them first—then burn them."

Dion smirked. "Finally, my powers are the setup instead of the punchline."

Ayana dodged another swipe from the Human like creature. "Whatever you two are doing—do it faster!"

Damien grabbed her hand. "We have to split them up."

Ayana didn't hesitate. "Lanelle! Dion! Take the wolf! We'll handle the creepy shadow guy!"

They broke apart, forcing the creatures to follow.

Lanelle and Dion tag-teamed the wolf, moving in sync. Dion kept it trapped in ice, slowing its movements, while Lanelle burned it down in pieces, forcing it to collapse bit by bit.

The creature howled, writhing, but Lanelle didn't stop until the flames engulfed it entirely.

Then, with a final screech, the beast collapsed into ash.

Dion grinned. "And that's how you exterminate night-mares."

Lanelle exhaled, shaking out her hands. "One down."

Meanwhile, Damien and Ayana had a bigger problem.

The Human like figure wasn't fighting them—it was summoning more shadows.

Black tendrils whipped outward, striking like living weapons.

Ayana dodged, grabbing Damien and pulling him behind a tree. "We can't fight it. It's not solid enough!"

Damien panted. "So what do we do?"

A sound cut through the chaos—stone grinding against stone.

Lanelle spun toward the pedestal. "It's still moving!"

The runes were glowing again, reactivated now that the wolf was gone.

Dion cursed. "Then we just have to keep this thing busy until it's done."

Ayana sprinted forward, grabbing the nearest thing she could—a branch still burning from Lanelle's fire.

She swung.

The moment the flame touched the Human like figure, it recoiled.

Damien's eyes widened. "The fire hurts it!"

Lanelle grinned. "Now we're talking."

She lifted her hands—and this time, the fire burned bright.

The shadows lurched backward, hissing, retreating from the light.

The pedestal shook violently.

And then—

A door appeared.

A circular stone entrance, embedded in the ground. The runes flickered once—

Then the stone rumbled open.

Ayana's chest heaved. "That's it. That's the way down."

The Human like figure let out an inhuman shriek. It lunged for them.

But the pedestal flared with golden light.

The force knocked the creature backward, sending it fading into the shadows once more.

Silence.

Lanelle wiped sweat from her forehead. "Tell me we never have to do that again."

Dion huffed. "I'd love to say yes, but something tells me it's about to get worse."

Damien gestured toward the open path. "Let's go before it changes its mind."

Ayana took a deep breath. "Alright. Time to find the core."

Knock, Knock—Oh Wait, It's a Trap

The air grew heavier as they stepped through the stone entrance, leaving the ruined clearing behind. The deeper they descended, the worse The Garden became. The walls of the tunnel shifted as they walked, the texture almost organic—roots curled along the surfaces like veins, pulsing with a faint, sickly glow. The air was thick, humid, laced with putrid undertones.

Dion ran a hand along the tunnel wall, then immediately yanked it back. "Yeah, okay, I hate this. The walls are breathing."

Lanelle squinted. "You're imagining things."

Dion frowned. "Nah. Feel it." Lanelle hesitated—then pressed her fingers to the nearest root.

It twitched.

She jerked back. "Oh, hell no."

Damien didn't stop walking. "Keep moving. If we're right, the core is down here."

Ayana glanced at him. "And if we're wrong?"

He didn't answer.

The tunnel spiraled downward, deeper than they expected. It shouldn't have been possible—The Garden itself wasn't supposed to be this big, but inside it…things didn't follow normal rules.

Lanelle slowed as they reached a fork in the path. "Left or right?" Dion tilted his head, listening. Both paths were silent—too silent.

Then, he heard it.

A heartbeat.

Not their own.

Faint. Steady. Coming from the right.

"This way," he muttered, leading them down the right tunnel.

As they walked, the light began to change. The glow in the walls dimmed, replaced by something...darker.

Shadows moved on their own.

The air thickened like it was fighting them, resisting their presence.

Then—

They saw it.

A door.

It was massive, ancient, built into the very foundation of The Garden. Unlike the crumbling ruins above, this door was untouched by decay. Dark stone, engraved with symbols none of them recognized, its surface glowed with a faint golden shimmer.

And right in the center—

A message.

Four must enter, but only truth will pass. Speak what is lost, and the heart shall open.

Ayana groaned. "Another riddle."

Dion squinted at the engravings. "Okay, so... 'Speak what is lost.' What does that mean?"

Lanelle frowned. "Something missing? Something taken?"

Damien ran his hand along the symbols, thoughtful. "Or something we lost."

They stared at the door, waiting for it to make sense.

But nothing happened.

Ayana sighed. "I swear, if we have to fight something again, I'm just gonna play dead."

Dion chuckled. "What's lost though? What's missing?"

Lanelle exhaled sharply. "Could be anything. Time. Memories. The Garden itself."

Damien looked at the twisting shadows along the walls. "Maybe...the truth?"

He turned to the door and spoke, voice steady. "Reveal the truth."

Nothing.

Dion crossed his arms. "Alright, that was a long shot."

Ayana tapped her foot impatiently. "What if it's something specific? Like a name. An event."

Lanelle frowned, deep in thought. "What if it's the original name of The Garden?"

The words hung in the air.

The moment she said it, the shadows trembled.

Dion's eyes narrowed. "Oh, we're onto something."

Damien turned to the door. "But we don't know its name."

Something moved behind them.

Lanelle spun around just in time to see the darkness at the edges of the tunnel shift—

A figure stepped forward. Not the shadow-creatures. Not the wolf-thing. Not the insect monsters.

This was worse.

It was unnaturally tall—stretched, distorted. Its limbs were too long, its head tilted at an unnatural angle. Its robes weren't cloth, but woven from shadows themselves, undulating like they were alive.

Its face was hidden beneath the void of its hood. But its eyes—those were visible.

Not glowing, not burning like the others.

Just empty.

Deep.

Endless.

Ayana felt her stomach twist.

"Tell me that's not who I think it is," Dion muttered.

The figure took a single step forward.

Its voice was soft, but filled the entire space.

"You do not belong here."

The shadows rushed toward them.

"GO!" Damien yelled.

They ran.

The tunnel collapsed behind them, the walls screaming as the vines closed in.

The light from the core flickered, then vanished completely.

And just like that—

The Garden threw them out.

They hit the ground hard, skidding back into the clearing.

The portal was gone. The silence was deafening.

Ayana coughed, shaking dust from her clothes. "Okay. That thing? That's new."

Damien let out a low breath. "I am so tired of being kicked out of that damn place."

Ayana sat up, rubbing her arms. "That wasn't just another creature. That thing—it was waiting for us."

Damien didn't say anything, he was still staring at the ground. Because when he'd hit the dirt, something had fallen out of his hand.

A single golden shard.

Small, barely the size of a coin. But pulsing faintly with the same light that had flickered behind the door.

Ayana noticed it first. "Damien…what is that?"

He picked it up slowly, turning it over in his fingers.

As he did, a whisper filled the air. Not from The Garden. Not from the figure. Not from anything else they had encountered before.

It was ancient.

Soft.

And it only said one word.

"Remember."

Damien's breath caught.

Dion sat forward. "Alright. Someone explain to me why the hell we just got evicted,"

Lanelle crossed her arms. "I don't know. But whatever that door was hiding?"

She looked at the golden shard in Damien's hand.

"We just got one step closer."

Buried in the Stacks

A yana's fingers curled around the golden shard, heart thudding in her chest. The word "Remember" flickering faintly across its surface, like a dying ember. The others had fallen into an uneasy silence, their eyes locked onto the shard like it might explode at any second.

Lanelle was the first to break it. "Okay. Well. That's new."

Dion leaned in slightly, squinting. "Yeah, and probably not a good sign."

Ayana swallowed, the weight of the moment pressing against her ribs. The Garden had rejected them, tossed them out like they were intruders, yet here it was—still reaching out.

"I don't get it," she muttered, running her thumb over the surface. It was warm, like it had been sitting in the sun all day. "What are we supposed to remember?"

Damien crossed his arms, brow furrowed in deep thought. "The message on the door—'Speak what is lost, and the heart shall open.' Maybe this is tied to that. Something's missing, something The Garden wants us to find."

"Awesome," Dion deadpanned, throwing his hands up. "So instead of solving riddles in The Garden, now we get to solve them out here, too? Love that for us."

Lanelle ignored him. "If this thing is reacting now, something must have triggered it. Could've been us talking about the door. Could've been whatever freaky magic you got going on," she added, nodding at Ayana.

Ayana shifted uncomfortably. She hadn't forgotten about the vine incident. The way the plant had moved toward her, like it was drawn to her, had been subtle, almost hesitant, but enough to confirm what she didn't want to admit.

Something had changed.

"I don't have magic," she said, a little too quickly. "I don't feel different."

Dion snorted. "Yeah? Tell that to the possessed tree."

Ayana shot him a glare, but before she could argue, the shard pulsed again.

A second word appeared beneath the first.

"Name."

Lanelle sucked in a sharp breath. "Oh. Oh, I don't like that."

Dion held up a hand. "Wait. So now it's 'Remember Name?' What does that even mean?"

Ayana stared at the glowing words, her mind racing.

A name.

A lost name.

A name that was forgotten.

Her pulse quickened. The Garden had a name. That's what she had said when they were at the door, when the shadows had shifted like they were responding to her words.

Damien exhaled sharply. "We need to find out what The Garden was called before it became...whatever it is now."

Ayana turned to him. "Don't you know?"

Damien shook his head. "My grandpa always called it 'The Secret Garden.' That's all I know."

Lanelle muttered under her breath. "And I'm guessing the

internet isn't gonna be helpful?"

Dion rolled his shoulders. "Doubt it. If this place was common knowledge, someone would've figured this out already."

Ayana turned the shard over in her hands. "So...where do we even start?"

For a moment, no one spoke.

Then, Damien straightened, something clicking behind his eyes. "There might be something. The library archives."

Lanelle made a face. "Don't tell me we're about to research."

Ayana shook her head, but the corner of her lips twitched. "Library's our best shot. Even if the name isn't on record, there might be something."

Damien nodded. "Then let's go. The sooner we find something, the sooner we get back in there and figure out what's really going on."

Lanelle sighed. "Alright. But if a shadow creature pops out of a history book, I'm burning this whole place down."

Dion clapped his hands together. "See, now that's the energy we need."

Ayana tucked the shard safely into her pocket, ignoring the way it warmed against her skin. She had the strangest feeling that whatever they were looking for—whatever name had been lost—wasn't meant to be found.

And yet, they were getting closer.

Too close.

And The Garden knew it.

Ayana had been in libraries before—normal ones, the kind with the low murmur of voices, the distant hum of printers, the rustle of pages. But this? Even the usual background noise—the creak of shifting chairs, the soft buzz of the fluorescent lights—felt muffled, distant. Like the air itself was pressing in, listening.

It didn't help that they were tucked deep into the archives, where the scent of old paper and dust clung thick in the air. The dim yellow glow from the overhead lamps barely pushed back the shadows curling between the towering bookshelves.

Dion flopped into the nearest chair with a dramatic groan. "I just want it on record that this is actual torture."

Lanelle, flipping through a heavy, leather-bound tome, didn't glance up. "Duly noted. Now shut up and help."

Dion sighed loudly, dragging the closest book toward him. The dust cloud it released made him immediately regret his decision. "Oh my God. This thing is older than my soul."

Damien was fully absorbed in a massive book of local legends. "If it gets us closer to the name, I don't care if you have to read a hundred old books."

Ayana ran a finger along the frayed edge of a discolored map. "There has to be something. If The Garden has been here for centuries, it had to be on a map somewhere. Right?"

Lanelle turned another page, her brows furrowing. "Unless it was erased."

A chill ghosted down Ayana's spine.

Dion lifted his head. "That's ominous."

Lanelle tapped the yellowed paper in front of her. "Think about it. We have been kicked out once, and y'all twice. The Garden doesn't want us finding answers. What if people before us tried to do the same thing?"

Damien's fingers tightened around his book. His voice was quiet, thoughtful. "I don't know if anyone outside of my family has ever been there. It's always just been me and my grandpa."

Dion cleared his throat. "So...worst-case scenario. If this place was wiped from existence, how do we find a name that no one remembers? I mean, it is magical, right?"

Lanelle sighed. "Then we look where no one else would."

They fell into a rhythm, searching through maps, records, old journals. Pages turned. Dust rose. Footsteps barely made a sound against the worn carpet.

Ayana felt herself slipping into a strange sort of focus, half-aware of the world around her, half-aware of the golden shard in her pocket.

It was warm.

Pulsing.

Like it knew they were getting closer.

Then—

Damien stiffened. "Wait." Everyone snapped their heads up as he turned the book toward them.

A newspaper clipping. Over a hundred years old, the ink smudged with age, but the words were still legible enough.

The headline read:

"Mysterious Land Sealed from Public—Local Authorities Refuse to Comment."

Dion let out a low whistle. "Okay, that's suspicious."

Damien skimmed the article. "It says there was an 'incident'—something that forced the local government to block access. They called it an 'unexplained phenomenon' and said the land was 'not safe for travel.'"

Ayana leaned over his shoulder. "That's it? No details?"

Damien turned the page,. "No. The report cuts off. It's just a bunch of blacked-out lines."

Lanelle muttered, "Nothing screams cover-up like redacted documents."

Dion sat back, arms crossed. "Alright. So something happened, and now it's buried. But if people used to be able to go in, that means the Garden wasn't always…I don't know, whatever it is now."

Damien's voice was quieter, like he was piecing things together. "Before this 'incident'… people came and went freely." His gaze flicked to Lanelle. "But after?"

The pieces clicked into place.

"Only my family could get in."

Ayana's stomach turned.

"That can't be right," Damien murmured to himself. "The Garden was supposed to be a gift. It was always meant to be open. So why close it?"

Dion tapped the page. "Better question—who closed it?"

A heavy silence.

Lanelle drummed her fingers against the book's spine. "Is there anything else? Did they name it?"

Damien's gaze dropped to the faded words. His expression shifted.

"…Yes. But part of it's smudged out."

Ayana's pulse quickened.

She grabbed the book, staring at the faded text.

There wasn't much left to read. But there was just enough to piece something together.

"E________________'s Veil."

Her heart skipped. "E-something Veil."

Lanelle frowned. "A name? A title?"

Dion tapped his chin. "Could be both. Veil sounds like a barrier. Maybe The Garden was meant to be…I don't know, a passage between two places?"

The golden shard flared hot. Ayana sucked in a breath, jerking her hand from her pocket.

Everyone felt it.

And then—

The lights flickered.

The hum of the air conditioning cut out.

Somewhere in the stacks, a book fell from the shelf with a soft thud.

Lanelle's body went rigid. "Nope. Nope, absolutely not."

Dion stood slowly. "Something is here."

Ayana's breath caught in her throat.

She felt it too.

A presence.

Watching.

From the far end of the archive, a shadow shifted.

Ayana stood abruptly. Her chair scraped against the floor. "Time to go."

No one argued.

They grabbed what they could and bolted from the archive, the feeling of unseen eyes following them the entire way.

And just before Ayana stepped through the library doors, she swore she heard a whisper.

Soft. Ancient.

"You were not meant to know."

Her heart slammed against her ribs.

She ran.

Buckets, Bad Omens & Booker's Bad Attitude

in the air. The bleachers were packed with students decked out in school colors, waving handmade posters, screaming chants. The Douglas High team had been waiting for this game all season, their first real challenge against an outside school. No secret missions, no special training—just straight basketball against Jefferson High, a regular, well-trained team that had no idea what kind of competition they were up against.

Damien bounced the ball twice against the court, his fingers light, his stance loose. His heart thrummed in his chest—not from nerves, but from anticipation. This was his court, his place to be free from everything else. Here, it wasn't about magic, mysteries, or hidden gardens. It was about the game.

Dion stood beside him. "Alright, I'm just saying—if we win by thirty or more, y'all owe me food."

Booker scoffed, adjusting his headband. "If we win by thirty, they better just hand us the state championship now."

Quashawn snorted. "We ain't winning by thirty. We winning by fifty."

Dion grinned. "I like your confidence."

"Five minutes till tip-off!" The announcer's voice echoed through the gym.

The Douglas team huddled up, their coach—a stocky, no-nonsense man with a permanent scowl—stood in the middle.

"Alright, listen up." Coach's voice was gruff, sharp. "Jefferson High is good—not great, but they hustle. They ain't gonna hand this game to you, so you better outwork them every damn second." His gaze locked onto Damien. "You lead the floor, understand?"

Damien nodded once, jaw tightening. "Got it."

Coach turned to the rest of them. "We push the tempo. Fast breaks, quick passes, no sloppy plays. If I see one of y'all getting lazy on defense, you're sitting."

Booker raised a hand. "What if we're just so good on offense that we don't need defense?"

Coach glared. "Then you're sitting first."

Dion snickered, clapping Booker on the back. "Walked into that one, bro."

"Alright, hands in," Damien said, bringing them into the huddle. Their palms stacked together, the weight of the moment heavy but electric.

"One, two, three—Douglas!"

The buzzer sounded, signaling the start of the game.

First Quarter

Damien stepped to center court, locking eyes with Jefferson's point guard—a tall, wiry kid with sharp features and an easy smirk.

"Y'all ready for this?" the guy taunted.

Damien just smirked. "We been ready."

The referee tossed the ball high into the air, and Quashawn launched himself up, tipping it cleanly to Damien.

Damien pushed the pace immediately, dribbling upcourt with tight control, his eyes scanning the defense. Jefferson's team shifted quickly, their center already sagging into the paint.

He swung it to Dion on the wing.

Dion faked left, crossed right, and pulled up for a jumper.

Swish.

The crowd exploded.

"Too easy!" Dion shouted, backpedaling on defense.

Jefferson pushed back hard. Their point guard moved fast, calling for a screen. Damien slid over it, staying glued to his hip, forcing a bad pass.

Booker snatched it and bolted.

Fast break.

One defender in his way. He slowed, took a step, then—

Bam. A behind-the-back pass to Quashawn, who caught it mid-air and slammed it down with authority.

The gym erupted.

Jefferson called timeout.

Quashawn jogged back toward them, grinning. "Told y'all. Fifty-point win incoming."

Second Quarter

Jefferson came out swinging after the timeout. Their defense tightened, forcing Damien and Dion into tougher shots. Their point guard started hitting threes, cutting the lead down to four.

Damien wiped sweat from his forehead. "Alright, they wanna fight? Let's fight."

Next play, Damien drove hard to the basket, drawing two defenders before kicking it out to Booker, who was wide open in the corner.

Booker hesitated, then—

Splash. Three-pointer.

He turned to the bench, grinning. "Call me Booker Curry."

Dion rolled his eyes. "I'm literally about to bench myself just so I don't have to hear that again."

Jefferson pushed again, their big man getting inside for an easy layup.

Damien snapped his fingers. "Tighten up!"

Quashawn and Booker clamped down in the paint, making Jefferson's shots harder. Dion started picking off lazy passes, and by halftime—

Douglas was up by twelve.

The gym was alive with the roar of the crowd and the rhythmic pounding of feet against the bleachers. Douglas High was already crushing Jefferson, the scoreboard flashing a comfortable lead, but the real show was just beginning.

Ayana took a deep breath as she stood on the edge of the court with Tariana and Jade. The rest of the dance team was lined up behind them, waiting for the signal. Tariana bounced on her toes, barely containing her excitement. "They're about to lose their minds."

Jade exhaled, tugging her ponytail tighter. "As long as we hit every move clean, they better."

Ayana scanned the crowd. The basketball team was seated in the front row, cooling off during halftime. Damien caught her eye, lifting his chin in silent support. She smirked and stretched out her arms.

The announcer's voice boomed over the speakers. "And now, to keep this energy going, make some noise for your Douglas High Dance Team!"

The gym erupted.

Then the music hit.

They moved as one, their steps crisp, precise, and powerful. Sneakers squeaked against the court, but the rhythm of their routine drowned it out. They glided through the first formation, bodies flowing seamlessly from one move to the next.

Tariana led the charge, stepping forward into a fierce hip-hop combo, every chest pop and sharp movement exuding confidence.

Ayana followed, her body moving effortlessly with the beat. Every turn, every step felt like second nature.

Jade spun into a flawless drop, flipping her ponytail at the perfect moment, drawing an even louder roar from the stands.

The team fed off the energy, riding the wave of cheers and flashing cameras.

A quick formation shift. They spread into a sharp diagonal, Jade, Tariana, and Ayana holding the front line.

The tempo picked up.

This was their moment.

Tariana stepped out first, hitting a sharp footwork sequence that sent the crowd into a frenzy.

Ayana rolled into a body wave before snapping into a controlled lock, her movements precise and fluid.

Jade brought the heat with a flawless spin into a low-level sweep, springing up just in time to land in sync with them.

The gym went wild.

Somewhere in the chaos, Damien's voice rang out. "That's my girl!"

Ayana barely held in a grin.

The music swelled, leading them into the final section. Their bodies moved in perfect harmony, every muscle trained to hit the last few beats with explosive energy.

One last drop. One final pose.

Boom.

They froze.

A perfect second of silence.

Then the noise crashed over them, deafening.

They stayed locked in place, letting the cheers soak in before finally standing, breathless and victorious.

As they jogged off the court, Tariana threw her arms up. "Oh, we ate that! Not a single crumb left."

Jade wiped sweat from her forehead, grinning. "That might've been our best performance yet."

Ayana grabbed her water bottle, buzzing from the rush. "They loved us."

Booker jogged past, dribbling a basketball with a smirk. "Y'all didn't just eat. You devoured. That other team might as well pack it up now."

Tariana crossed her arms. "I wouldn't blame them."

Damien appeared beside Ayana, his expression glowing with pride. "I don't know how I'm supposed to focus on the second half after that."

She smirked, bumping her shoulder against his. "You better. We still gotta win this game."

He chuckled, shaking his head. "No pressure, huh?"

The buzzer rang, signaling the end of halftime. The basketball team huddled together, preparing to dominate the second half. The dance team filed back into the bleachers, still high off the adrenaline.

Ayana sat down, taking a sip from her bottle as she tried to settle her racing pulse. Then something strange prickled at the back of her mind.

She glanced toward the far end of the gym, where the crowd had thinned near the exit doors.

There.

A figure stood in the shadows, just beyond the doors.

Not a student. Not a teacher. Not a regular fan.

A chill crept through her bones. The figure didn't move. Didn't react. It was just watching. Then, just as quickly, it was gone.

Ayana turned quickly, her eyes locking with Lanelle's from across the gym. Lanelle had seen it too. Her jaw was tight, her expression unreadable.

"Did you see that?" Ayana mouthed.

Lanelle's eyes flickered to the doors, then back to her.

"Yeah," she mouthed back. "I saw it."

Ayana swallowed hard. The game continued. The crowd cheered. The night moved on.

But deep down, she knew—

Something was wrong. And it was just getting started.

Third Quarter

They broke Jefferson. Dion picked off a pass and immediately tossed a full-court dime to Damien. Damien caught it in stride. One defender in front of him.

A split-second decision.

He spun, elevated, and laid it in—smooth.

The crowd went crazy.

Jefferson tried to answer back, but Quashawn blocked their shot so hard the ball bounced into the stands. "Oh yeah, y'all done." Quashawn laughed, flexing.

Jefferson's coach called another timeout.

Dion turned to Booker. "Alright, twenty-point lead. You buying food?" Booker shrugged. "Game ain't over yet."

Fourth Quarter

Jefferson looked gassed. Their shots fell short. Their defense was slower.

Damien controlled the pace, dictating every move. Dion and

Booker pushed the tempo, hitting shot after shot. Quashawn owned the paint, grabbing rebounds like his life depended on it.

And then—

The dagger.

With two minutes left, Dion caught the ball, stepped back, and drilled a three-pointer from deep.

Nothing but net.

The crowd lost it.

Jefferson's heads dropped.

They knew it was over.

Final Score: Douglas 82 – Jefferson 54

As the buzzer sounded, Damien let out a breath, a slow grin spreading across his face.

They did it.

The crowd rushed the court, students cheering, chanting. Ayana and Lanelle were screaming from the bleachers.

Dion patted Damien's back. "Not bad, Cap."

Quashawn draped an arm over Booker. "So, about that food…"

Booker sighed, rubbing his temple. "I hate all of y'all."

Dion laughed. "Fine, I'll be generous. Lanelle and Ayana buying too."

Lanelle, passing by, snorted. "Oh, absolutely not."

Damien looked around the gym, the crowd, his team, the scoreboard still flashing their win.

For the first time in a long time, there were no mysteries. No magic. No shadows creeping behind them.

Just basketball.

And it felt damn good.

* * *

The cafeteria was nearly empty, long cleaned out from the post-game rush, but that didn't stop the Douglas High crew from taking over the space like it was their personal VIP lounge. There were leftover nachos from the concession stand, a few bottles of soda had mysteriously appeared, and Tariana had somehow convinced Booker to let her control the aux. The playlist was a mix of old-school bangers and fresh hype songs, bass rattling off the cafeteria walls.

Ayana leaned against Damien's shoulder, half-listening to Dion and Quashawn arguing over who had the better stat line.

"I had six steals," Dion was saying, pointing aggressively at Quashawn. "SIX. That's defense. That's elite."

Quashawn scoffed, shoving another handful of fries into his mouth. "Steals don't count if you turn it over two seconds later."

Booker snickered. "Ain't no way you let him cook you like that."

"I DIDN'T turn it over," Dion protested, throwing his arms up. "Y'all just haters."

Jade, who had decided she wanted to hang, sighed, stretching her legs onto an empty chair. "It's way too late for y'all to still be talking about the game."

Tariana turned up the music, waving her hands like a DJ. "We need a break from all that. Let's get back to the real priority—vibes."

The group laughed, settling into the easy comfort of a win and a well-earned night off. It felt normal. No training, no missions, no magic.

Then the energy shifted.

It wasn't obvious at first. Just a glance, a flicker of something unreadable across Booker's face when the cafeteria doors swung open again, and Jalen walked in.

Lanelle had invited him, casually, like it wasn't a big deal. But the moment he entered the room, that familiar tension settled in, thick like humidity before a storm.

Jalen smiled as he slid into the group like he belonged there. Because technically, he did.

But Booker didn't look at him.

Ayana noticed the way Lanelle's posture shifted slightly, like she could already feel Booker watching without even turning his head.

Dion, being Dion, clocked it in two seconds flat. He arched an eyebrow, glancing between them. "Oh, this is about to be fun."

Lanelle shot him a look. "Mind your business."

Dion grinned. "It *is* my business. This is premium entertainment."

Jalen, either oblivious or choosing to ignore it, sat next to Lanelle, draping an arm along the back of her chair like it was the most natural thing in the world.

Booker looked up, just for a second.

Just long enough for Ayana to see it—that quick flash of something in his expression. Not anger. Not jealousy, exactly. But something sharp, something quiet.

Lanelle's fingers tapped lightly against her knee, like she felt it too.

Before anything could settle, before the conversation could turn awkward, the first weird thing happened.

The overhead lights dimmed for half a second too long.

Lanelle glanced up, eyebrows drawing together.

"Yo," Dion groaned, throwing a fry at Booker. "Turn down the damn air conditioning, man. It's freezing all of a sudden."

Booker, who was nowhere near the thermostat, threw the fry back. "Dude, it's literally the same temperature it was five minutes ago."

"No, it's not," Tariana muttered, rubbing her arms. "It got cold."

Lanelle did not look convinced.

The cafeteria doors creaked open.

No one had touched them.

For a moment, the group fell silent.

Then, Booker let out a low laugh. "Alright, which one of y'all invited Casper?"

Quashawn stood up, shaking his head. "Y'all overreacting. It's just the building settling or some sh—"

A sharp, single, hollow knock echoed through the space.

Knock.

It came from the far side of the cafeteria—the doors that led to the back hall of the school, where the janitor's closet and storage rooms were.

Everyone froze.

"...Please tell me y'all heard that," Ayana said slowly.

Dion turned his head toward the sound, his face unreadable. "Oh, I heard it."

Jade sighed dramatically, standing. "Alright, let's not do the horror movie thing where we just stare at the creepy noise and wait for something to grab us."

Tariana snorted, shaking off the tension. "Yeah, I vote we relocate before something possesses Booker."

Booker looked genuinely offended. "Why me?"

"Spirits love trash-talkers," Ayana said, slinging her bag over her shoulder. "And you're the MVP."

The group shuffled out, laughter strained. Lanelle lingered, her gaze snagging on the doors. She swore—just for a second—because there - just for a second - a shadow slithered across the floorboards, too liquid to be human.

She walked faster.

The dorm lounge offered false comfort—cracked couches, a vending machine buzzing like an angry hornet, and cologne so thick it choked the air. But at least there were no creepy sounds—just the hum of soft music and the occasional laugh.

Except...

Booker sat apart, jaw clenched, scrolling his phone like it owed him money.

Jalen leaned closer to Lanelle, voice low. "You good?"

She blinked. "Yeah. Why?"

Jalen's gaze flicked briefly to Booker, then back to her.

"You just seem...off."

She forced a smirk. "Just tired."

Jalen's hand brushed lightly against her knee—a small, fleeting gesture. Lanelle glanced up, Booker was looking.

Dion, who had been watching the whole exchange like a TV drama, exhaled loudly. "Y'all got some nerve acting like I don't have super-hearing."

Tariana groaned. "Okay, absolutely not. If we're doing this weird tension thing, I'm gonna need a drink first."

Ayana threw a pillow at her. "You're drinking Sprite."

Dion snickered, but then—

A chair scraped against the floor.

Loud. Sudden.

No one had touched it.

Everyone froze.

Jalen suddenly looked very awake. "...Was that—"

Lanelle stood abruptly. "We're not doing this again."

Dion was staring past them, at the window reflection. There were too many people in the reflection.

Lanelle noticed.

So did Ayana.

This is Not A Drill... Except It Totally Is

The fluorescent lights buzzed overhead like irritated wasps as Lanelle slid into her usual seat in Covert Ops & Protective Tactics, pulling out her notebook even though she knew today wouldn't require taking notes. The practical exercises were always unpredictable, and she had a feeling this one was going to be a mess.

Agent Halloway, their instructor, stood at the front of the classroom, her arms crossed over her tactical vest. The woman rarely smiled, and when she did, it usually meant someone was about to fail spectacularly.

"Listen up," she said, clicking the remote in her hand. The screen behind her flickered to life, displaying a series of surveillance photos—cafés, subway stations, hotel lobbies, city streets filled with people oblivious to the fact that they were being watched.

"For the next two weeks," Halloway barked, "you'll babysit a target in the wild." She paced around the room. "Your objective? Complete an active protection detail in a civilian environment. One of you will be assigned as the protector, the other as the client. Throughout this exercise, you will face multiple test scenarios meant to challenge your ability to protect without detection." She paused her steps back at the front of the room. "Blend in. Or fail."

Lanelle perked up. *Finally, something hands-on.*

"You will not know when, where, or how a threat will be introduced. Your job is to keep your client safe without drawing attention. You must learn to predict danger before it happens. If your target is compromised, you fail. If your cover is blown, you fail. If I so much as catch one of you looking over your shoulder like you're expecting trouble? You fail."

A few students murmured, but Lanelle barely reacted. The whole point of the exercise was to blend. People who looked paranoid stood out. People who acted too careful made it obvious they had something to protect.

Halloway continued, clicking to the next slide—a list of evaluation points.

Success Criteria:

- The client must remain safe at all times.
- The protector must stay within reasonable proximity without making it obvious.
- You may not use direct contact or intimidation unless absolutely necessary.
- You may not reveal your cover, even to "emergency responders."
- You must adapt to and de-escalate live test threats without engaging in a direct fight unless authorized.

The instructor's gaze swept across the room, pausing briefly on those who had a bad habit of being reckless.

"Some of you have already been in combat classes and think protection is about eliminating threats," she continued. "You are wrong. A good operative prevents a situation before it escalates. You will use situational awareness, quick thinking, and deception to keep your client safe. No unnecessary action. No dramatics."

A few students exchanged glances. No dramatics? This was going to be a challenge.

Halloway pulled out a stack of folders and began calling names.

"Sparks, you're with Benjamin."

He didn't look at her right away, just stretched his arms behind his head before finally glancing in her direction.

Lanelle arched a brow. "Try to keep up."

Booker smirked, but whatever he was about to say was cut off.

"Everyone, take a folder. Inside you'll find your assigned locations, potential threat profiles, and detailed schedules. You will follow these precisely, just like a real protection detail. Your movements will be monitored, and your interactions will be reviewed."

Lanelle opened the envelope, scanning the contents. Their assignment was set in a small city district about an hour away. A mix of open and closed environments—coffee shops, a bookstore, an outdoor park, even a social event at a small venue. It was a real-world test of different situations, requiring them to adapt on the fly.

She skimmed further down the page.

Known Threats:

- Petty theft/potential mugging scenario.
- Pickpocket attempts.
- Tail surveillance.
- Simulated kidnapping attempt.

Booker whistled low under his breath, looking over the same information. "Cool, cool. Casual abduction attempt. Love that."

Lanelle shut her folder. "At least you're not the one responsible for keeping me safe."

"Yet," he shot back, grinning. "I'll get my turn."

Her jaw tightened slightly. She *really* didn't want to think about how that would go.

Halloway cleared her throat. "Final rule—if either of you fail, your *partner* fails with you."

That got everyone's attention.

Lanelle's stomach tensed. Now, it wasn't just about passing on her own skill. Booker's success—or failure—was now tied to her.

Booker exhaled, running a hand through his hair. "Guess we better not screw this up, huh, Nell?"

She glared at him, but he just smirked, completely unbothered.

Halloway tapped the whiteboard once, cutting through the noise. "You start tomorrow. Dismissed."

Lanelle closed her folder with a sigh, her mind already running through possible scenarios. She had two weeks to prove herself.

Two weeks to make sure Booker didn't screw this up for her.

And two weeks to ignore the nagging feeling in her gut that said working this closely with him was going to make *everything* more complicated.

* * *

The hum of computers filled the dimly lit classroom, blue light bouncing off sleek black desks as students settled into their seats. *Cyber Surveillance & Digital Recon* was one of the most advanced courses at the academy, and Dion loved every second of it.

This was his domain—the place where secrets weren't stolen with a lockpick or a hidden camera but extracted from encrypted servers and buried behind layers of false identities.

Imani, seated next to him, was less enthused. She had one earbud in, idly scrolling through her screen. She was in the class because she was good at it, not because she particularly enjoyed spending hours staring at lines of code.

Damien, on Dion's other side, looked like he was merely tolerating the lesson's existence.

Their instructor, Agent Heartings, paced in front of the room with his usual air of no-nonsense authority. "Alright, listen up," he called out gruffly.

The monitors flickered. A live feed of security cameras from around the world filled the screens. A crowded subway station. A dimly lit café. A hotel lobby. A government building's entrance.

"Today's exercise," Heartings continued, "is a real-time surveillance challenge. Each of you will be assigned a target, and your job is to track them. Gather intel. Identify potential threats. And most importantly—remain undetected."

Dion grinned, cracking his knuckles. "Oh, this is gonna be *good*."

Damien sighed. "You sound way too excited about this."

"Bro, this *is* the game. What's better than knowing things you're not supposed to know?"

Heartings ignored them. "Your data packet will contain limited information—name, last known location, known associates. Your job is to *fill in the blanks.* If you trip a security alert, get locked out, or alert your target, you fail. No do-overs."

The classroom buzzed as their screens refreshed with new assignments.

Dion scanned his file:

TARGET: L. Kessler

Location: Downtown Metro Station

Objective: Identify travel route & track communication activity

Damien muttered, scrolling through his own. "Mine's in a hotel lobby. Low-key, I feel like we're training to be professional creeps."

Imani sighed dramatically. "*Thank* you. Finally, someone says it."

Dion smirked. "Nah, this is precision information gathering. Y'all just don't have the vision."

She arched a brow. "Or maybe I just don't *love* digging through people's personal lives for fun."

"That's why you got me, babe. I do the illegal things, and you get plausible deniability."

Imani rolled her eyes but didn't argue.

Dion got to work, pulling up the metro's security feed first. It was easy—too easy, considering this was supposed to be a controlled exercise. His target, L. Kessler, was right there, mid-thirties, wearing a dark green jacket, holding a newspaper like he was starring in a spy movie from the 80s.

"Alright, Mr. Kessler," Dion murmured. "Where you headed?"

Damien frowned at his own screen. "My guy is making a call in the hotel lobby," he hesitated. "Yo, can we tap into the call log?"

"I already did," Dion said, fingers flying over the keys. "But here's the weird thing—this dude's phone is bouncing off *scrambled* towers. And he just sent an encrypted text right after the call."

Imani leaned over, scanning his screen. "Why would a *fake* target need military-grade encryption?"

Dion didn't have an answer. Heartings—who never *ever* let them break from the lesson—looked up, watching their screens a little too closely.

Something wasn't right.

Damien ran a cross-check on his target. The file was vague. Too vague.

Dion tapped into a database, trying to run Kessler's past movements.

He found nothing.

Not missing records. Not gaps in the timeline.

Like the dude *didn't exist.*

"...Imani?" Dion said slowly.

She was already ahead of him, scanning another system. Her expression darkened. "This isn't normal."

Then the classroom's emergency lights kicked on.

The main screen at the front of the room flickered. Red text bled across screens:

UNAUTHORIZED TRACE DETECTED. SYSTEM LOCKDOWN INITIATED.

Dion's stomach dropped.

"Oh," he muttered. "Oh, *hell.*"

Damien straightened. "That's *not* part of the simulation."

Imani's fingers hovered over her keyboard. "...Dion, what did you *do*?"

Dion's mouth went dry. "I *might* have tripped something."

Heartings didn't react immediately. He just tilted his head slightly, like he'd expected this.

The classroom door unlocked with a sharp *click.*

And a voice—calm, cold, and very much *not* pre-recorded—filtered through the speakers.

"Whoever's in my network," the voice said, smooth as glass, "you have *five seconds* to log out before I track *you.*"

A chill ran down Dion's spine.

Imani turned to him, whispering, "Get *out.* Now."

Dion didn't need to be told twice. His fingers flew over the keys, closing programs, wiping logs, erasing every trace of his presence.

The warning flickered again.

TRACE FAILED. DISCONNECTING.

The system went dark.

And then, everything returned to normal.

Silence stretched across the room.

Heartings clapped once. "Class dismissed."

The students hesitated before gathering their things, murmuring about what the *hell* just happened.

Dion, Damien, and Imani remained frozen in their seats.

Heartings finally turned to them, his expression unreadable. "A lesson for you all," he said, voice even. "If you go digging in the wrong places—"

Dion finished, voice hollow. "Something digs back."

Heartings smirked. "Exactly."

Imani let out a slow breath, closing her laptop. "I *hate* this class."

Damien grabbed his bag, muttering, "Next time, let's not *accidentally* start cyber warfare."

Dion barely heard them. Before the system shut down, he'd

seen a message typed directly onto his screen.

Nice try, kid.

His blood ran cold.

He looked at Imani.

She was already staring at him.

"…We are *so* telling Lanelle," she muttered.

Spy School Is A Scam

Lanelle's dorm had become the unofficial gathering spot that night. Ayana was perched on the bed, flipping idly through a textbook she wasn't actually reading. Damien and Quashawn were playing a half-hearted game of cards on the floor. Dion was scrolling through his phone, occasionally smirking at whatever ridiculous meme Imani had sent him. Tariana had taken over Lanelle's beanbag chair, stretching out dramatically while sipping from a stolen bottle of Gatorade.

Jalen perched on the desk's edge, knee jittering like a live wire. Booker lingered by the wall, arms folded, gaze sharpening every time Jalen's hand brushed Lanelle's chair.

Ayana speared a fry from the takeout spread in front of them, barely paying attention as Dion and Quashawn debated stats from the game—again. Tariana, across from her, had her chin propped on her palm, clearly zoning out.

Dion's grin split the room like a knife. "Place is so tense, I could bounce a quarter off it. Who's cracking first—Jalen, Booker, or Nell's self-control?"

Lanelle didn't even look up from her phone. "You shouldn't."

Dion gasped dramatically, clutching his chest. "Wow. A direct hit."

Tariana sighed. "What tension?"

Dion pointed blatantly at Lanelle, then at Booker, then back at Jalen. "That tension. The one everyone's pretending doesn't exist."

Booker finally looked up, his gaze flat. "Ain't no tension, bro."

Dion smirked. "Really? So if I just—" He made an exaggerated reach toward Lanelle's phone like he was going to read whatever she was texting. Instantly, she yanked it away, shooting him a glare.

Jalen laughed, draping his arm across the back of her chair in a way that was *too casual*. "Man, you stay messy."

Dion grinned. "It's a gift."

Booker's jaw flexed, a muscle twitching as Jalen's arm grazed Lanelle's shoulder. He didn't blink.

Ayana, who had been watching this unfold like a spectator at a reality show, leaned closer to Damien. "Oh yeah. This is premium drama."

Damien snorted. "You want popcorn?"

Tariana waved a hand. "Y'all making too much out of nothing. Maybe Jalen and Lanelle are chill. Maybe Booker's unbothered. Maybe Dion is just stirring the pot for fun."

Dion grinned. "See? She gets me."

Lanelle finally put her phone down, fixing Dion with a look. "You're being irritating."

"Yet, you still love me," he shot back.

Jalen, still relaxed but now looking ever so slightly smug, stretched his arms. "Yeah, it's funny how that works."

Booker made a noise in the back of his throat.

Quashawn, who had been mostly focused on his game with Damien, finally tossed his cards onto the floor with a groan.

"Forget all that. Can we talk about how school is trying to murder us? Because I'm one assignment away from faking my own disappearance."

Tariana rolled her eyes. "Please. You don't even have the discipline to disappear. You'd get bored and come back before lunchtime."

Quashawn shot her a glare. "First of all, disrespectful. Second, my schedule is insane! Coach has us in practice at dawn, then I got tactical conditioning, then econ—which, by the way, is the most unnecessary class—*then* I gotta study for two different combat assessments." He flopped onto his back. "This school is built different."

Tariana groaned, throwing an arm over her face dramatically. "You think you got it bad? My dance schedule has officially crossed into actual torture. We have morning conditioning, lunchtime drills, afternoon rehearsals, and *still* Coach has the nerve to say we're 'not sharp enough.' Like, ma'am, I have blisters on top of my blisters."

Booker smirked. "So dramatic."

Tariana peeked out from under her arm and pointed at him. "You try hitting six back-to-back routines in two hours and *then* sit through an advanced Physics lecture. I bet you'd start seeing God."

Dion snorted. "Yeah, Physics *is* disrespectful. But personally, I'm thriving."

Lanelle gave him a dry look. "You nearly caused an international incident in class."

Dion shrugged. "*Allegedly.* And in my defense, how was I supposed to know I hacked into a *real* surveillance feed? It was supposed to be a simulation!"

Damien shook his head. "The system literally warned you."

"Yeah, but like…I thought it was part of the exercise!" Dion grinned, looking far too pleased with himself. "Heartings just said 'gather intelligence.' He didn't specify *legal* intelligence."

Imani smacked his arm. "This is why I'm always stressed."

Dion threw an arm around her shoulders. "Nah, you love me."

Imani sighed. "Against my better judgment." She leaned into him, relieved that he started to warm up to her again.

Jalen, who had been watching the conversation with amusement, finally chimed in. "Alright, but for real, y'all got nothing on me. Y'all ever had to explain *calculus-based espionage strategy* to a dude who still thinks PEMDAS is a government agency?"

Ayana blinked. "Why would anyone need calculus for espionage?"

Jalen threw his hands up. "That's what I *said!* But apparently, trajectory calculations, velocity adjustments, and 'mathematical probability of success' are all things I need to *manually* calculate in the field. You know, instead of just doing what works."

Booker smirked. "That's because you rely too much on instinct."

Jalen met his gaze with a smug grin. "That's because my instincts are better than yours."

Booker's smirk tightened just a little, his posture stiffening slightly.

Lanelle, already tired of whatever this was, cut in. "Yeah, I'm with Jalen on this one—this school over complicates *everything*. Like, I'm in an actual *babysitting class.*"

Dion snorted. "It's called 'Protective Detail,' Nell. Not babysitting."

"I have to walk around with Booker for two weeks pretending like I'm some high-profile security guard," Lanelle continued as ignored him. "Meanwhile, I *also* have to stay up studying for my Covert Interrogation midterm because apparently, 'accidentally giving myself away' counts as 'failing the assignment.'" She sighed, rubbing her temples. "Oh, and let's not forget—if Booker screws up, *I* fail."

Dion's grin widened. "Oh, I *love* this."

Booker shrugged. "I mean, I'm feeling pretty confident about this. You worried about keeping up, Nell?"

Lanelle's glare was sharp enough to cut through metal.

"I'm taking bets on when she knocks him out," Dion stage-whispered to Ayana.

Ayana smirked. "Oh, I'd pay to see that."

Booker chuckled, completely unbothered. "Y'all act like I'm the one who's gonna mess up."

Jalen leaned forward slightly, resting his arms on his knees. "Yeah? What's your strategy, then?"

Booker glanced at Lanelle before shrugging. "Easy. Keep her safe without her noticing."

"So you *think* she wouldn't notice?"

Booker smirked. "I know she wouldn't."

Lanelle exhaled through her nose. "Oh my God, both of you *shut up.*"

Tariana, who had been watching like a soap opera, finally sat up. "Okay, but back to *me*. Did I mention I have three tests next week *on top* of a performance? I swear, this school is actively trying to break us."

Quashawn waved a hand. "They *are* trying to break us. That's kinda the whole point."

Damien, who had been quiet, finally spoke. "Honestly? I

don't even know what I signed up for half the time anymore. Between strategy simulations, combat evaluations, and mission prep, I don't even have time to breathe."

Ayana gave him a look. "You literally fell asleep standing up in class yesterday."

Damien sighed. "I *thought* it was a drill."

Dion whistled. "Y'all are really out here suffering."

Imani side-eyed him. "You are *also* suffering. You just enjoy the chaos."

"Facts."

Jalen stretched, cracking his neck. "Alright, so we've established that all of us are dying. But what's the move? Are we just accepting our fate or are we gonna cheat the system?"

Ayana smirked. "Define 'cheat.'"

Booker shook his head. "No. I already don't trust where this is going."

Dion sat up. "I'm just saying—if we *happen* to gain access to the faculty scheduling server and *accidentally* delay a few tests—"

Imani smacked the back of his head. "No."

Dion winced. "Ow, woman! Let me dream."

Damien sighed, rubbing his face. "I hate that I considered it for a second."

Lanelle stood, stretching. "Well, *I* have to go prepare for my fake bodyguard duties. Unlike some people, I actually take my training seriously."

Booker smirked. "You're gonna miss me by the end of this."

Lanelle rolled her eyes. "I'm going to shoot you with a tranq dart."

Tariana groaned. "If you do, *please* wait until I have popcorn."

As the group started leaving, Dion clapped his hands together. "Alright, great talk, team. We're all barely hanging on, everything is awful, and yet somehow, *I'm still thriving.*"

Imani tugged his ear. "Thrive your way into studying for your hacking exam."

"I regret everything," Dion groaned.

"You lovebirds done?" Jalen laughed, standing.

"She's bossy," Dion huffed.

Imani smirked. "And yet, you keep coming back."

Dion grinned. "Damn right."

"Alright, I'm kicking y'all out." Lanelle glanced at her watch.

"Good," Quashawn nearly ran to the door. "I need sleep before I have to pretend to care about Algebra in the morning."

Ayana waved dramatically as she walked out. "Don't fail your babysitting gig, Lanelle!"

"If Booker gets kidnapped, *please* let me know first," Dion called over his shoulder.

Booker just grinned. "Don't worry. I'll be fine."

Lanelle exhaled, watching as he left with the others, her mind already racing through all the ways this assignment was going to make her life hell.

She had two weeks of close proximity, two weeks of working side by side.

And she wasn't sure if she was dreading it more because of the mission—

Or because of *him.*

Nelly, We Have a Problem

L anelle adjusted the comm in her ear, barely resisting the urge to sigh as she trailed a few paces behind Booker through the bustling city district.

She didn't know why she had an issue with this. Was it really the assignment, or was it the fact that she was spending so much time with *Booker*?

They could be friends, right? It wasn't *weird* that they were stuck together for two weeks straight while she was *technically* seeing where things went with Jalen. That's all that was happening. It wasn't serious. They were just *enjoying each other's company.*

She smiled slightly, hearing that exact phrase in Jalen's voice in her head.

The whole point of this exercise was to blend in—to move unnoticed while keeping her "client" safe. *That* was what she needed to focus on.

Booker, however, was making that really difficult.

"You're walking like a bodyguard." Booker stuffed his hands into his pockets, glancing sideways at her. "Subtlety, Nelly. Ever heard of it?"

She arched a brow. "I *am* your bodyguard."

"Yeah, but you're supposed to be *subtle* about it. You look like you're two seconds away from suplexing a grandma."

Lanelle frowned. "Super what?"

"Never mind," Booker chuckled. Just relax. Act like we're *friends*."

Something in her stomach twisted. "Aren't we friends?"

Booker hesitated for a second. But then he smirked, glancing at her over his shoulder. "I don't know these days."

"Huh?" she asked, but he had already turned back around.

Booker gestured lazily at the surrounding shops. "What, you think someone's gonna roll up on me between DH Coffee and the pretzel stand?"

"Knowing this school? I wouldn't be surprised," she muttered.

Their assignment specified they needed to be out and about during class time, roaming through public spaces. Since there weren't any *streets* on campus, she assumed they were expected to move through open areas—quads, walkways, the commons—not sit in one place.

The academy's exercises weren't predictable. *Anything* could happen at any time. She had to constantly be watching, anticipating danger before it even looked like danger.

Booker, on the other hand, looked completely relaxed, strolling through campus like he didn't have a care in the world.

"See, *this* is what I mean," he said, casually dodging a guy on a scooter. "You're all tense. You gotta loosen up a little, *Nelly*."

She barely twitched at the nickname, but her jaw tightened. "I'll loosen up when this assignment is over."

He gave her a look. "Right, because this is about the mission."

She ignored him. *Of course it's about the mission. Isn't it?*

She wasn't thinking about how close he was. She wasn't thinking about how much easier everything was when she *wasn't* around him. And she definitely wasn't thinking about how Jalen had texted her that morning, asking if she wanted to grab coffee after her assignment ended.

She was focused.

And then, just as she was about to tell Booker to keep moving—

Something shifted, like the air around them had changed.

Lanelle's instincts flared.

She slowed slightly, scanning the crowd. People passed by in a blur of motion—nothing immediately suspicious. But something *felt* off.

"Alright, so, real question," Booker said, completely un-aware. "How mad would you be if I just—"

Lanelle grabbed his wrist and yanked him to a stop.

His eyebrows shot up. "Damn, at least buy me dinner first."

"Shut up." Her grip tightened. "I think we're being fol-lowed."

He turned his head slightly, his movements just subtle enough to not be noticeable. "How sure?"

"Eighty percent."

"Not ninety?"

"If I was ninety, we'd already be running."

He exhaled, nodding. "Alright. Play it out."

She let go of his wrist, adjusting their pace. They needed to be careful. She *hated* not knowing any other details about the assignment—no list of specific threats, no clear objective beyond "protect the client."

Booker slid his hands back into his pockets, playing it cool. "Where?"

"Three o'clock. Grey hoodie. Walks like he's got nowhere to be but somehow stays close enough to hear every word we're saying."

Booker smirked. "Sounds like a fan."

Lanelle ignored him, adjusting her earpiece. "Checking for a second tail."

They weaved through the crowd, slowing just enough to see if the presence behind them adjusted. Lanelle flicked her gaze across campus, toward the first-year building, spotting another figure.

Too still. Too focused.

"...We've got two."

Booker gave the barest nod. "Okay. What's the play?"

They moved seamlessly into a more crowded area, slipping between groups of students. Lanelle's pulse thrummed, not from fear, but from calculation. *Think ahead. Set the trap before they spring it on you.*

She steered Booker toward Howard Hall. If they could get into a space with fewer people, they'd get a better read on their followers.

They stepped through the entrance and she glanced behind them.

Pivoting sharply, she stepped between Booker and the incoming threats. One of them—a tall man with a sharp jawline and a scar above his eyebrow—smirked slightly.

"You're good," he admitted. "Most people don't clock us that fast."

"What do you want?" Lanelle kept her stance neutral.

Scar Brow tilted his head, his gaze flicking to Booker. "Not you."

Booker raised an eyebrow. "Wow. Rude."

"Too bad," Lanelle didn't relax.

The second guy shifted, hand twitching toward his pocket.

She moved before he could. She threw her barrier up, surrounding Booker and she stepped forward, grabbed his wrist, and twisted—just enough to make him wince.

Scar Brow raised his hands slightly. "Easy, easy. We're just here to talk."

"You don't tail someone if you just want to *talk*."

Booker leaned against the hallway wall. "Yeah, I mean, personally? I prefer *not* being followed around campus, but hey, that's just me."

Scar Brow exhaled, clearly weighing his options.

Lanelle tightened her grip on the other guy's wrist. "Try to pull a weapon, and I'll break it."

"...Fine," Scar Brow said finally. "Maybe next time."

Then, without another word, he gestured to his partner, and just like that—they backed off.

Lanelle didn't move until they were out of sight. Only then did she release the guy's wrist and step back.

Booker let out a low whistle. "Damn. I knew this would be fun."

Lanelle rolled her eyes. "Shut up."

Booker chuckled but didn't push it.

They went through the rest of the hour, and despite herself, Lanelle lightened up. Talking to Booker was easy, almost annoyingly so. He had this way of pulling her into conversations without her realizing it, making her forget—for a little while, at least—about the fact that they were technically on an assignment.

"In what universe are superhero action movies *not* the best ones?" Booker gawked at her, looking personally offended.

Lanelle shrugged. "I mean, I watched them when it was Dion's turn to pick movie night, but they're not really my thing. Just not my type of action movie."

Booker clutched his chest like she had physically wounded him. "Not your type? *Not your type?* You mean to tell me that you—Lanelle Sparks, a student at *this* academy, whose entire *life* is basically a spy movie—don't like superhero action movies?"

"That about sums it up."

"What's your type, then? Romance?" he teased, a smug grin tugging at his lips.

Lanelle gave him an incredulous look. "*Romance can have action in it.*"

Booker threw his hands up, scandalized. "*NO!* That's not how that works!" he yelled dramatically, causing a couple of people across the quad to glance their way.

Lanelle giggled, her amusement bubbling up despite her best efforts to keep it at bay.

Her phone vibrated in her pocket. Automatically, she pulled it out to check the screen.

Jalen: *Or are you having too much fun with Booker?*

Her smile fell.

Her fingers hovered over the keyboard. She typed out a response, then deleted it. Typed something else. Deleted that too. Then, sighing, she shoved the phone back into her pocket without replying at all.

When she looked up, Booker was watching her with a raised eyebrow.

"Everything okay?" he asked, his usual cocky demeanor giving way to something quieter.

Before she could answer, her comm buzzed in her ear, the

sharp voice of their instructor cutting through the channel.

"All protection teams, listen up. Your client will now be faced with a dynamic threat. This is a live scenario, and you are expected to respond accordingly. You won't know when or where, but the test begins *now.* If you fail to neutralize the threat without exposing your cover, you *both* fail."

Lanelle immediately straightened, every thought about Jalen vanishing from her mind.

Booker whistled low under his breath, stretching his arms behind his head like he was *thrilled* about whatever was coming next. "Oh, *this* is about to be fun."

She side-eyed him. "We have very different definitions of fun."

"Nah, you love it."

She ignored him, scanning their surroundings. They were in the middle of a the Quad.

The academy wasn't going to make this obvious. It could be *anyone.* A fake mugging. A planted device. A tail. Something subtle, but calculated. Their instructors were testing their ability to anticipate danger *before* it struck.

Lanelle's mind immediately shifted into strategy mode.

"We need to move," she muttered, adjusting her pace.

Booker matched her stride, shoving his hands into his pockets, playing an unbothered civilian. "Alright, boss. What's the call?"

She scanned the area again, looking for anything out of place. "If they're testing situational awareness, they're going to use something we won't immediately suspect. Which means we need to—"

They both heard it at the same time. It sounded like cries.

As they scanned their surroundings Booker took off, dashing

towards a little girl.

What the heck, Lanelle mumbled as she followed him "You need to stay with me," she hissed.

When Booker reached the little girl, he knelt and placed a hand on her shoulder. "What's your name?" he asked.

This was obviously a part of the assignment because why is a child in the middle of the quad. "Booker," she hissed again.

The little girl glared at her, then lifted her arm, and sprayed something into Booker's eyes. He dug his palms into his hands groaning in agony.

Lanelle's eyes got wide and the little girl turned and ran away.

"I told you to stop," she hissed. "It was a part of the dang assignment,"

"It's mace or something," Booker said between grunts.

"Stand up, I need to get you out of here." She scanned her surroundings. Everyone in the quad was going on like usual. This was Deceptive High after all. They were used to crazy stuff happening.

She needed to get him back to her room. Howard was the closest and there would be privacy there. She his arm and yanked up. As soon as she looked down, something hit her from behind.

She threw her barrier up, protecting her from hitting the ground hard. She dropped it immediately remembering she cannot use magic but the person who hit her, a tall man - *with a scar* - lifted his eyebrow.

She jumped to her feet. "Booker. Danger." Lanelle barely had time to process what just happened before Scar Brow lunged at her again. She sidestepped, barely dodging the grab, her pulse spiking. *Alright. So this wasn't just about protection—this was a full-on combat scenario.*

Great.

Booker, still groaning and blinking rapidly, stumbled to his feet. "You coulda warned me," he hissed, rubbing at his burning eyes.

"I *did* warn you," Lanelle shot back, circling her opponent. "But *nooo*, you had to go sprinting towards the *obviously* planted little girl like you were some kind of hero."

"My bad for having *instincts*," Booker grumbled.

Scar Brow smirked. "You two always bicker this much?"

Lanelle didn't answer. Instead, she feinted left before pivoting sharply, driving her elbow into his ribs. He grunted, but recovered fast, grabbing her wrist, and twisting.

Shit—

She used his own momentum, dropping her weight, and flipping him over her shoulder. He hit the ground hard, rolling before springing back up. He was good. But she was better.

Booker, meanwhile, was still trying to clear his eyes. "Nelly, I can't see, but I *can* hear you flipping people. Please tell me we're winning."

Lanelle blocked a punch, gritting her teeth. "We're working on it."

Scar Brow came at her again, faster this time. She ducked under his swing, twisting to land a sharp kick to the side of his knee. He staggered but didn't go down.

"Not bad," he admitted.

"Not done," she corrected.

He smirked, reaching into his jacket. Lanelle's instincts screamed at her—*weapon.*

Booker might have been temporarily blind, but he wasn't useless. The moment he heard the shift in Scar Brow's stance, he lunged—completely by muscle memory—and tackled the guy before he could pull anything.

"Got 'im!" Booker grunted.

"You *tackled* him?" Lanelle asked, incredulous.

"Bro tried to cheat," Booker shot back, pinning Scar Brow with his forearm. "We don't play fair against cheaters."

Scar Brow grinned, despite being restrained. "Good instincts."

Before Lanelle could blink, a sharp whistle cut through the air.

Scar Brow immediately went limp.

Booker froze. "...Did I just kill him?"

Lanelle rolled her eyes. "No, idiot. That's our signal."

Sure enough, their comms buzzed again, and their instructor's voice filtered through. "Sparks, Benjamin—exercise complete. Well handled."

Booker slowly let go, sitting back on his heels. Scar Brow exhaled, shaking his head as he got up. "You kids are fast learners."

Lanelle crossed her arms. "We adapt."

Scar Brow cracked his neck. "You hesitated before neutralizing the threat."

"I was assessing."

"Assessment could get your client killed."

Lanelle's jaw clenched. She knew that.

Booker, now blinking slightly clearer, finally turned to her. "You good?"

"I'm *fine*." She shook out her hands, still buzzing from the fight. "Let's go."

Booker stood, rubbing his shoulder. "You sure? Because I feel like you have some unresolved tension you might wanna talk about."

Lanelle exhaled sharply, already walking away. "You *always* think I have unresolved tension."

"Because you *do!*" he called after her.

Scar Brow chuckled. "You two are gonna have *fun* working together."

Lanelle flipped him off over her shoulder.

Booker snickered, falling into step beside her. "Oh yeah, this is gonna be *great.*"

She groaned. "Two weeks. *Two weeks* of this."

"C'mon, Nelly," he grinned. "You love me."

She glanced at him, catching the teasing in his expression. He wasn't completely wrong.

But he didn't need to know that.

So she just shook her head and kept walking.

I Swear, Dion, If We Die—

Lanelle was exhausted.

The kind of exhaustion that settled into her bones and made her want to collapse face-first into the nearest bed, couch, or even semi-soft carpet if it came down to it. Training had been brutal today with Dion. On top of the babysitting stuff with Booker and swimming, she was dead.

So when she and Dion finally made it back onto campus grounds after trudging through the thick forest that surrounded the academy, all she could think about was making it to her dorm and getting off her feet.

Dion, however, had other plans.

He wasn't walking like someone who had just endured three hours of hand-to-hand combat drills and being blasted by fire. No, he had that particular bounce in his step—the one that meant he had something on his mind.

Lanelle sighed. "No."

Dion turned his head toward her, frowning. "I didn't even say anything."

"You didn't have to." She adjusted the strap of her training bag over her shoulder. "Whatever dumb idea you're cooking up, the answer is no."

Dion clutched his chest dramatically. "Wow. So little faith in me."

She shot him a side-eye. "You *stole* a campus golf cart last week."

"Technically, I *borrowed* it."

"For an off-campus Boba run?"

"I *returned* it."

She pinched the bridge of her nose. "Dion—"

"Look, this isn't about golf carts or Boba," he interrupted, nudging her with his elbow. "I found something."

Lanelle exhaled slowly. "Dion—"

"No, seriously," he pressed, his voice dipping just enough to be serious. "I *actually* found something. Something weird."

That got her attention. She stopped walking and faced him fully.

"...Weird like *what*?"

He jerked his head toward the east part of campus, the less-trafficked part of campus. Most students cut through the quad to get to the dorms, but Dion was pointing toward the older buildings.

"I was on my way back from—"

"Breaking rules?"

"—minding my business," he corrected, "and I noticed something off."

Lanelle sighed. "You always notice something off."

He gave her a knowing look. "Yeah. And when's the last time I was wrong?"

She opened her mouth to counter that but immediately closed it.

Damn it.

"Fine," she muttered. "What did you find?"

Dion grinned, already leading the way.

Lanelle followed, despite every ounce of common sense telling her to keep walking toward her bed.

The air changed the deeper they went into the East wing. It wasn't something most people would notice. But they weren't most people.

Lanelle felt it in the way the air thickened, like it was pressing against her skin.

Dion flicked his fingers, signaling for her to stop. His posture shifted, eyes closing as he tuned in.

She stayed still, watching him, waiting.

His sonic hearing kicked in, sending out ripples through the space like an invisible radar. Heartbeats, soft footsteps, the faintest scratch of fabric shifting—Dion caught everything.

Then, he activated his X-ray vision. Lanelle watched as his expression shifted from focused to alarmed.

"Uh...okay, yeah. Something's definitely in there." His voice dropped, but there was an unmistakable edge to it.

Lanelle tensed. "How many?"

"Two people. Standing still. No movement." Dion's brows furrowed. "They're just...staring at something."

That was never a good sign. Lanelle activated her thermal vision.

The world around her shifted. Colors bled into reds, oranges, and yellows. Heat signatures pulsed against the colder background, showing her the warmth of bodies even behind walls.

And just like Dion said—there were two people.

Except...something else stood out. A third heat source. But it wasn't human. It was burning hot—too hot. Magic.

"There," she whispered, pointing. "There's something radiating heat in the center of the room."

Dion's eyes flicked to her. "That's where they're looking."

They reached the far end of the hallway, where a heavy wooden door stood slightly ajar.

Lanelle frowned. "This part of the building is supposed to be closed off."

"Exactly," Dion said. "So tell me why there's a light on inside."

Lanelle leaned in slightly, peering through the gap in the door. The room beyond was dim, barely lit by the flickering glow of a single hanging bulb. But what caught her attention wasn't the light.

It was the faint shimmer in the air. Magic. Not their magic. Something else.

Lanelle's breath hitched.

"That's not normal."

"No," she murmured. "It's not." She pushed the door open the rest of the way.

Inside, the space looked like an old study room—desks pushed to the sides, bookshelves lined with forgotten texts.

But at the center of the room was a large, polished stone table.

Resting in the middle of it was a jagged black stone throbbed with an eerie glow, casting fractured shadows that seemed to writhe like living things. Dion let out a low whistle. "Okay. That's definitely weird."

Lanelle moved closer cautiously, every muscle tense.

It wasn't just a rock. Magic radiated from it, subtle but undeniable. The air around it shimmered, bending light unnaturally. Dion tilted his head. "Think it's dangerous?"

Lanelle shot him a look. "Do you ever ask that before dragging me into things?"

"Not really."

She sighed, stepping closer. The moment she did, the glow

brightened.

Dion frowned. "Uh, did you do something?"

The glow from the stone pulsed brighter, casting eerie, flickering shadows against the walls. Lanelle's fingers itched to throw up a barrier. Something told her that making any sudden movements would be a bad idea.

Dion, however, had zero patience for staring contests.

He tilted his head, sonic hearing still active. "They know we're here," he whispered.

A chair screeched across the floor. One of the figures in the room finally moved.

A woman stepped into the dim light, her silhouette solidifying from shadow. Her hair was silver, pulled back into a sleek ponytail, and she was dressed in dark tactical gear—not a student. Definitely not a teacher either.

The second figure emerged behind her, a tall, stocky man with sharp eyes that flicked between them, calculating. He looked like someone who didn't just fight but enjoyed it.

Lanelle glanced at Dion. He caught her look and gave her the subtlest nod.

The woman's eyes narrowed, gloved hand hovering near her belt. "You're not supposed to be here."

Lanelle let out a dry laugh. "Funny, I was just about to say the same thing."

Dion leaned casually against the doorframe. "So, what's the deal? You two lost or something?"

The man crossed his arms, expression blank. "Walk away."

Lanelle raised an eyebrow. "See, the problem with that is…" She gestured at the very suspicious glowing rock.

The woman sighed, shaking her head. "This doesn't concern you."

Dion snorted. "We go to a spy school. Everything concerns us."

The woman glanced at her partner. "I told you they'd be a problem."

Lanelle took a step forward. "I'm really hoping that's not a threat, because I'm gonna be honest—I'm not in the mood."

The man's stance shifted, feet spreading slightly. Lanelle recognized it immediately. He was preparing for a fight.

Dion must have caught it too, because his posture changed instantly.

Lanelle flicked her fingers, subtly summoning a small flame between them—not an attack, just a warning.

"Okay, let's not get stupid," Dion said lazily, but there was a sharp edge to his voice. "We don't know what that rock does, but I'm guessing you do."

The woman's jaw tightened.

Lanelle took another step forward. "So how about you explain?

The man moved first. Before he could lunge, she snapped her fingers—her fire expanded instantly, sending a bright flash across the room. The heat forced the woman and man to stumble back, momentarily blinded.

Dion acted fast, using the distraction to unleash a sonic pulse. The air rippled, the deep frequency vibrating through the room. The shelves rattled, books tumbling down as the pressure knocked both figures off balance.

"Move!" Lanelle shouted.

Dion darted toward the table. His X-ray vision scanned the rock—its structure wasn't normal. Something inside it was shifting, pulsing like a heartbeat. Definitely magic.

The woman recovered fast. "Idiots," she hissed, pressing a

device on her wrist.

The stone flared.

Lanelle barely had time to react before a wave of cold, foreign magic pushed her back. It wasn't fire. It wasn't ice. It was something else.

The force ripped through her chest, sending her skidding backward. Dion caught her before she could hit the ground.

The air around the rock shimmered violently.

"We need to go. Now." Dion's voice had lost all humor.

Lanelle gritted her teeth. Retreat wasn't her style.

The woman smirked. "Smart choice." Lanelle burned that smirk into her memory.

They weren't done here. Not even close.

With one last look at the shuddering, pulsing rock, Lanelle and Dion turned and ran.

* * *

The natatorium was packed with students, teammates, and families, their voices bouncing off the high ceiling. The sharp tang of chlorine filled the air, grounding Lanelle in the moment.

She stood on the starting block, rolling her shoulders, stretching out her arms, forcing her muscles to stay loose even though every nerve in her body was coiled tight. One breath. Just one.

She had trained for this. She had pushed her body to its limits, but she hadn't mastered it yet. Not completely.

Her eyes flicked toward her competition. Taylor and Stephanie; Douglas Academy's fastest swimmers. They stood on their own blocks, adjusting their goggles, shaking out their limbs, completely locked in.

She sucked in a deep breath, steadying herself—

"LET'S GO, NELLY!"

Dion's voice boomed over the crowd.

Lanelle's head snapped up toward the stands, her glare locking onto her twin brother, who was standing up, gripping the railing, acting like this was his race.

"DON'T CALL ME THAT!" she yelled back.

Quashawn, leaning next to Dion, threw his head back, laughing. "She's in the zone, y'all! Focus up, champ!"

The official's whistle pierced through the noise. The announcer's voice echoed through the speakers. "Swimmers, take your mark."

Lanelle dropped into position, gripping the edge of the block.

The pool stretched ahead, the water like glass. Fifty meters. No air. She could do this. She would do this.

BEEP.

She launched.

The second her body hit the water, the world above disappeared.

The chaos of the crowd, the heat of the lights, Dion being obnoxious—gone. It was just her and the water.

Reach. Pull. Kick.

Every stroke was sharp, powerful. Her legs moved like pistons, driving her forward.

The burn in her lungs started early, but she ignored it. She had felt this before. She had trained past this feeling.

She wasn't coming up.

Halfway.

Keep going.

The ache in her chest sharpened, her body desperate for oxygen.

No.

Her vision blurred slightly at the edges. The pool floor tiles streaked past.

She was gaining.

Taylor was still ahead, but not by much.

Three-quarters.

Her lungs screamed. The fire in her chest clawed upward.

Just a little more.

Just a little—

Her vision swam.

And then, before she could stop herself—

She broke the surface.

No.

She gasped, coughing, her chest heaving as she gulped in air.

She had lost momentum.

That moment of hesitation cost her. Taylor's fingers slammed into the wall first.

Lanelle surged forward, desperate, her fingertips grazed the wall a heartbeat too late. Second place. Again

The moment she ripped off her goggles, her eyes snapped to the scoreboard.

Final Results

🥇 Taylor - 1st Place

🥈 Lanelle - 2nd Place

🥉 Stephanie - 3rd Place

So. Close.

A loud, dramatic "OH, COME ON!" rang out from the stands.

Lanelle didn't even need to look.

Dion.

He sounded personally offended.

She pressed her forehead against her arm, still catching

her breath, the water dripping down her face mixing with frustration.

She had been right there.

Jalen was the first to reach the edge of the pool, grinning. "Lanelle, that was insane! You almost had her!"

"Exactly," she muttered. "Almost."

Dion jumped down the stairs, pushing through the crowd like he was about to protest the results. "Are you serious?! You were like— a hand away!"

Lanelle sighed, pulling herself out of the pool.

"I was watching the whole time, and I swear you were ahead for, like, a second, and then—boom, betrayal."

"It's called needing to breathe," Lanelle muttered, tugging her swim cap off and flicking it at him.

Tariana jogged up, nudging Lanelle's shoulder. "Hey. Second place. You literally just swam against two of the fastest people here and almost beat them."

Lanelle didn't answer.

She could still feel that split second where she broke the surface. The moment her body betrayed her.

Taylor walked over, shaking water from her arms, her expression unreadable. Lanelle braced for a cocky remark.

But instead, Taylor tilted her head. "You almost made it the whole way, didn't you?"

Lanelle blinked.

Taylor wasn't mocking her. She was acknowledging her.

Slowly, Lanelle exhaled, her competitive frustration settling. "Yeah. Almost."

Taylor grinned. "Next time, huh?"

Lanelle smirked. "Next time."

Taylor gave her a nod before walking off, and Lanelle turned back to her crew.

Jalen tossed her a towel. "You know, for a second there, I thought you had it."

"Me too," Lanelle admitted, toweling off her face.

Dion crossed his arms. "You did have it."

Lanelle glanced at him, expecting another loud declaration of injustice. But for once, he wasn't joking.

"You're one second away from first place, Nelly," he said.

She rolled her eyes, but she knew what he meant. This wasn't a loss. It was proof. She was one second away.

Next time....she wasn't stopping.

The Thing About Glowing Rocks (And Bad Ideas)

The thing about almost winning was that it left a bad taste in Lanelle's mouth.

She wasn't obsessed with it. Not really.

But every time she shut her eyes, she could feel the water again, the moment she broke the surface too soon, the fraction of a second that had cost her first place.

Dion, of course, made sure she never forgot.

"You were one second away, Nelly," he had told her, more than once.

Like she didn't already know that.

But second place wasn't even the thing keeping her awake at night.

Because three days ago, she saw a glowing rock on one of Dion's shenanigans.

And two people—people who definitely weren't students or teachers—had been watching it.

Then the rock disappeared. And nobody else seemed to notice.

And that was something Lanelle couldn't let go.

Which explained why, instead of getting some much needed rest, or doing research to help Damien and Ayana with The

Garden, she was currently sitting at one of the farthest tables in the library, sifting through books so old the pages felt fragile.

This was not how she planned to spend her week.

Across from her, Dion was completely useless.

He had his feet kicked up on the table, spinning a pencil between his fingers, flipping through a book with absolutely no effort to actually read it.

Lanelle turned a page and sighed. "You can go, you know."

"Nah." Dion flipped another page, not even looking at it. "I wanna see where this goes."

She glared. "You're not helping."

He grinned. "I am! Moral support."

Lanelle pinched the bridge of her nose. "I hate you."

"I love you too," he said cheerfully.

The library of Douglas High was a place that demanded silence, with its impossibly high shelves, dim lighting, and deep mahogany wood that made everything feel older than it should be. Most students only came here if they had to. Lanelle had never been one of those students.

Dion stretched, tossing his book onto the pile of completely ignored research. "So, what exactly are we looking for?"

"Anything on magical artifacts that react to people," Lanelle muttered, flipping another page.

Dion blinked. "That's...vague. Why don't we just call Mom?"

"I want to see if I can figure it out on my own," she snapped.

Dion hummed, tapping his fingers against the table. "So, that means..."

"We have to go off what we do know," Lanelle finished.

Dion grinned. "Which is that two very suspicious people knew exactly what it was."

Lanelle exhaled. "And they took it."

Dion leaned forward. "Okay. So then, real question—who the hell were they?"

That was the thing she couldn't figure out.

The woman—silver hair, dark tactical gear—had moved with precision. The guy—stocky, solid—looked like someone waiting for a fight.

They weren't random intruders. They had been sent. Which meant that someone knew about that rock.

Worse...they were trying to keep it hidden. Lanelle hated not knowing things.

Dion tapped the table. "Alright, I'll bite. If we're not getting answers here, what's the plan? Calling Mom?"

"No," she finally answered. "We go back."

"I'm sorry, we what?"

She looked up. "We go back to the room. We missed something."

Dion stared at her. "Lanelle. Do I need to remind you that last time we were in there, we got blasted across the room by spooky rock magic?"

She crossed her arms. "We weren't ready."

Dion looked personally offended. "I was plenty ready! I just—" He waved a hand vaguely. "Didn't expect the rock to try and kill us."

"Exactly." Lanelle leaned forward. "So now we know what we're dealing with. And we can actually investigate."

Dion groaned. "You're the worst."

She smirked. "You're still coming."

Dion sighed dramatically. "Of course I am. You'd die without me."

Lanelle rolled her eyes.

*****

The hallways were too quiet in the East Wing. The overhead lights flickered just enough to make it feel like a horror movie waiting to happen.

Lanelle moved carefully, her senses on high alert. Dion walked beside her, silent, for once.

When they reached the door to the study room, Lanelle paused.

She pressed a hand against the wood. Her fingertips glowing faintly to the warmth, tying her abilities to the rock's energy.

It was warm. "Dion."

Dion immediately focused. His posture shifted as he activated his sonic hearing.

He closed his eyes, listening. "No heartbeats. No footsteps. But..." His brow furrowed. "Something's still humming."

Lanelle exhaled. "On three?"

Dion grinned. "You read my mind."

One.

Two.

Three.

She pushed the door open. The room looked the same.

Mostly.

The glow was gone, but at the center of the table, there was a single folded piece of paper.

Dion frowned. "That wasn't there before."

Lanelle stepped forward and picked it up. She unfolded it, her pulse spiking—

Then she froze.

It was a message. *You should have left it alone.*

A chill ran down her spine. Dion let out a low whistle. "Welp. That's ominous."

Lanelle swallowed.

She exhaled, fingers tightening around the note.

Dion grinned. "Oh, yeah. We're definitely in this now."

Lanelle folded the note and stuffed it into her pocket.

One thing was certain.

They weren't leaving this alone.

IV

The Lies That Built This Place

Secrets, Surveillance, and Unwanted Socializing

Lanelle couldn't shake the feeling that someone was watching her.

It wasn't paranoia—not exactly. But after finding that note in the east wing, everything felt heavier. More tense, like something was lurking under the surface, waiting.

Which was exactly why she and Dion had agreed on one rule: No one else gets involved.

Which meant no talking to the crew. No face-to-face discussions. No obvious moves.

And if Deceptive High was good for anything, it was making sure its students had all the tools necessary to be very, very sneaky.

By lunchtime, they had a game plan:

- Step 1: Check school records for unknown personnel.
- Step 2: Scan security footage for any suspicious activity.
- Step 3: Set up surveillance taps in key locations—hallways, exits, staff rooms.
- Step 4: Do not, under any circumstances, get caught.

Dion had managed to access last week's visitor logs, but there were no new faculty hires, no listed visitors, no names they didn't already know.

Which meant whoever those two were, they were either fake identities, deep undercover, or ghosts.

By mid-afternoon, they had slipped into one of the unused security rooms—a dark, cramped space filled with glowing monitors and outdated tech. Rows of security feeds flickered on the screens, different angles of the school captured in black-and-white.

Dion pulled out a sleek, hacked access device and plugged it into the system.

"Alright," he murmured, fingers flying over the keyboard. "Let's see if our mystery guests left us anything useful."

Lanelle leaned in, watching as footage from the past week sped across the screen.

Students coming and going. Teachers lingering. Nothing out of the ordinary.

"There," she pointed. Dion rewound the footage. The east wing hallway. Two figures, blurry, barely visible. The timestamp was two hours after they had left.

The intruders had come back. Dion exhaled. "Okay. That's creepy."

They watched as the two figures moved carefully, avoiding cameras when possible, slipping into the same room where the rock had been.

Then—

One of them looked up, directly into the camera. Lanelle's stomach tightened. It wasn't just a glance. It was a knowing look.

The footage cut to static. Dion swore. "They wiped it."

Lanelle sat back, hands clenching. "Which means they knew

we'd come looking."

Dion tapped the keyboard frustratedly. "I might be able to restore it, but they're good."

As he typed, Lanelle started wondering who these people were Why were they there? Did they want her or Dion or did they stumble upon something they shouldn't have?

"Got it," Dion's voice brought her out of her thoughts.

Lanelle focused on the computer. The grainy video continued with Silver hair and her companion walking up to the rock. It was still glowing and they seemed to have something on their hands.

"Look," she said pointing. Dion stopped the video "What?"

"They got gloves or something on," she said.

Dion managed to zoom in on the rock and Silver hair had leather gloves on.

"Can she not touch them?" Lanelle asked.

"There goes that bracelet she had on right before she blasted us, you remember?" Dion asked. "She touched it right before."

Lanelle leaned in and squinted. "Yea, whatever pulse came from that."

They went through the video a few times.

"We still don't know who they are," Lanelle said.

"I got that covered."

Dion turned his attention to the computers. A few moments later he had – absolutely nothing.

He banged his fists on the table in frustration. "They are no one, nobody. I can't find them."

Lanelle exhaled. They needed another angle. She pulled out her phone and, against her better judgment, opened the group chat.

Lanelle: Need info on school security systems. Who's available?

Jalen: ...Why?

Lanelle: Just answer the question.

Jalen: I'll see what I can dig up.

Booker: Why are we being vague??

Dion: Because it's more fun this way.

Lanelle shut her phone before Tariana could ask too many questions.

"Tariana's gonna kill me if I don't answer her," she muttered.

Dion grinned. "Oh, absolutely." Lanelle groaned. She had too much going on to deal with that right now.

But Tariana wasn't the kind of person who took silence well. And by that evening, she had officially had enough.

* * *

Lanelle sprawled across the plush sofa, a lazy smirk curling her lips as she reached for another chocolate from the glass bowl on the coffee table. She popped it into her mouth with a satisfied hum. "So tell me again why we're not out causing chaos tonight?" she asked, her dark curls tumbling over her shoulder.

"Because," Tariana drawled from the floor, where she lay on her back, "for once, we deserve a night where we're not running, scheming, swimming, or dancing. Just one."

"Mmm." Ayana, perched by the window, propped her chin on her hand. "I don't know. I kind of like the running and scheming."

Tariana rolled her eyes. "We all need a night without routines, or laps, or—" she lowered her voice conspiratorially, "love triangles."

Lanelle's head snapped up, eyes narrowing. "First of all—"

"What's going on with you and Jalen anyway?" Ayana cut in before she could finish. "You two have been spending a lot of time together. Are y'all dating? And what about Booker?"

Lanelle blinked, thrown off by the rapid-fire interrogation. "Dang, one question at a time."

Tariana smirked. "Nope. We ask them all, and you answer one at a time."

Lanelle exhaled through her nose, rubbing her temple. "Jalen and I are not together. We're just hanging out, seeing where things go. And Booker and I—we're friends. We're in a good place."

Tariana made a skeptical noise, pursing her lips. "According to who? You, or him?"

"According to us," Lanelle said firmly.

"Absolutely not," Ayana said.

Both Lanelle and Tariana turned to her.

"What do you know?" Lanelle asked slowly, suspicion creeping into her tone.

Ayana hesitated, then broke under the weight of their stares. "Damien told me—" she sucked in a breath, "and that means y'all better not tell—but Damien told me that at practice one day, Dion was talking about tension between Jalen and Booker. Booker said there was no tension, just that he was trying to get back on your good side. They went back and forth, and Booker ended up admitting he was in it for the long haul." She took another breath before dropping the bomb: "He said he'd be there when you got over Jalen and came back to him."

The room fell silent.

Lanelle's expression was unreadable. Tariana watched her carefully. Ayana pressed her lips together, bracing for the fallout.

"Well, damn," Lanelle muttered.

"Do you want to get back with Booker?" They asked at the same time.

Ayana frowned. Tariana, however, groaned in exasperation, then launched into an explanation of what had gone down last year. "Lanelle made Dion forgive Imani, but now she won't forgive Booker."

"But Dion acts like he hates her every time she's around," Lanelle shot back. "I don't want to act like that with Booker."

"He used to do that," Tariana pointed out. "Not anymore. They're fine now."

"And you and Booker are 'friends,'" Ayana said, making exaggerated air quotes. "Which means y'all skipped that stage."

Lanelle hesitated, uncertainty gnawing at her. She didn't know what she wanted.

A sharp knock at the door saved her from answering.

"Let me in!" Jade's voice called from the other side.

Tariana got up to open the door, and Jade sauntered in, followed by Taylor and Stephanie.

"Your brother said y'all were having a girls' night, so I thought I'd crash," Jade said, dropping onto the couch.

"We crashed her crash," Taylor said, laughing. "We overheard Dion."

Jade kicked off her shoes and plopped onto the couch next to Lanelle, stretching her legs across her lap like she belonged there. "Alright, what's the gossip? Y'all looked way too serious when we walked in."

Lanelle nudged her legs off with a huff. "Nothing. Just Ayana running her mouth."

"I was not running my mouth," Ayana said, tossing a pillow at her. "I was sharing valuable information."

Taylor snorted. "That sounds like running your mouth."

Stephanie grinned, setting down her bag. "Well, I hope y'all weren't planning on keeping things serious, because I brought reinforcements." She unzipped the bag and pulled out snacks, a deck of cards, and a bottle of contraband soda—off-limits at the school but always somehow making its way into their nights.

Jade clapped her hands. "Now this is the kind of girls' night I signed up for."

Tariana grabbed the cards. "Alright, let's start with something light before we get into the real chaos. Truth or Dare, but make it interesting."

"Define interesting," Ayana said suspiciously.

"No weak truths. No easy dares. We're going all in," Tariana declared, shuffling the deck with ease.

Lanelle smirked. "I like where this is going."

Jade leaned forward, already invested. "I'll go first. Ayana, truth or dare?"

Ayana sighed, knowing she was doomed either way. "Dare."

Jade's grin widened. "Perfect. I dare you to sneak down the hall, grab the biggest pillow from the common room, and get back here without getting caught."

Ayana groaned. "We're really starting with breaking the rules?"

Lanelle raised a brow. "You scared?"

Ayana shot her a look, then stood up dramatically. "Fine. But if I get caught, I'm dragging y'all down with me."

As soon as she slipped out, the room filled with laughter and whispers as they took bets on whether she'd get away with it.

"She's gonna trip over something," Taylor said confidently.

"Nah, she's got this," Stephanie countered.

A few minutes later, Ayana burst back in, slightly out of breath but victorious, hugging an oversized pillow to her chest. "Boom!"

Jade cackled. "Okay, okay, respect."

Ayana tossed the pillow at her. "Now it's my turn. Tariana, truth or dare?"

Tariana arched a brow. "Truth."

"Boo!" Jade complained.

Ayana ignored her. "Okay, who was the last person you thought about kissing?"

Tariana, for once, looked flustered.

"That's a good one," Lanelle said, crossing her arms.

Tariana paused before answering. "Nope. I'm switching to dare."

Jade clapped. "Uh-uh, no switching!"

"She's switching, which means she doesn't want to answer," Taylor teased.

"Fine," Ayana said, rolling her eyes. "Then your dare is to text him and say you were just thinking about him."

Tariana gave her an unimpressed look. "You are the worst."

Ayana grinned. "And yet, you love me."

As Tariana begrudgingly picked up her phone, the rest of the girls cackled and leaned in to watch.

The night stretched on with more ridiculous dares, over-the-top truths, and uncontrollable laughter. At some point, Taylor convinced them to play a dramatic reenactment of their most embarrassing moments, and Lanelle, despite herself, ended up in tears from laughing too hard.

By the time they were sprawled out on the floor, surrounded

by snack wrappers and tangled blankets, the tension from earlier had completely faded.

Stephanie yawned. "This was exactly what I needed."

"Same," Tariana admitted, stretching. "We should do this more often."

Jade smirked. "Well, I crash the best parties, so just let me know."

Lanelle sighed contentedly, staring up at the ceiling. "Yeah… for one night, it's nice not having to worry about anything."

Tariana turned her head toward her with a knowing look. "Told you."

For the first time in a while, everything felt easy.

And for tonight, that was enough.

Veil of Shadows, Heart of Light

The cool night air bit at Ayana's skin as they rushed out of the library, their hurried footsteps echoing against the stone pathways. No one spoke. No one dared. The weight of the whisper still clung to her ears, lingering like a ghostly presence just behind her.

They didn't stop until they reached the small courtyard nestled between the dorms, the soft glow of the campus lanterns barely cutting through the dark.

Dion bent over, hands on his knees, catching his breath. "Okay. Someone please tell me we all heard that."

Lanelle ran a hand through her hair, her expression set somewhere between disbelief and exasperation. "Oh, we heard it."

Damien turned back toward the library, eyes scanning the empty pathway. "It didn't follow us."

"It doesn't have to. It knows we know," Ayana shivered.

They stood there for a moment. The name—E's Veil—had triggered something. The Garden knew they were getting close. And it didn't like it.

"So," Lanelle started, arms crossed. "Do we talk about how we just got haunted in the archives or do we move on like that didn't just happen?"

Damien's jaw tightened. "We don't have a choice. We need to figure out what 'E's Veil' means."

Dion let out a dry laugh. "Right, because clearly, messing with the unknown is going great for us."

Ayana ignored him, turning her focus on Damien. "Is there anything in your family's records that mentions a veil? Anything at all?"

"Nothing I can remember, but I can check my grandfather's old journals," Damien shook his head. "He documented everything about the Garden."

Lanelle exhaled, glancing back at the looming structure of the library. "I'm guessing we're not going back in there anytime soon."

"Nope." Dion popped the 'p' for emphasis. "Not unless we want to get cursed."

A silence settled between them before Ayana finally broke it. "Then we need a new plan."

They reconvened in Damien's dorm room, where he pulled out a battered wooden chest from beneath his bed. The scent of old parchment and aged leather filled the room as he carefully unlatched the lid and began sifting through stacks of handwritten notes, maps, and faded photographs.

"This is everything my grandfather ever wrote about the Garden," Damien murmured. "If there's anything about its original name, it has to be in here."

Dion skimmed through a stack of loose papers, pausing as he pulled out a drawing. "Hey, check this out." He held up an old ink sketch of a grand archway, overgrown with vines, the entryway dark and endless. Beneath it, a note in elegant script read:

The Veil guards the path. Only the knowing may pass.

Ayana inhaled sharply. "That's it."

Lanelle peered closer. "So 'Veil' isn't just a poetic name—it's an actual barrier."

Damien's fingers tightened around the journal in his hands. "And the only way past it...is knowing."

Dion frowned. "Okay, but knowing *what*?"

Ayana's heart pounded.

* * *

The entrance to The Garden loomed before them, its once-vibrant colors muted, the air thick with something almost suffocating. The ancient trees now stood eerily still, their branches twisted like skeletal fingers.

"We shouldn't be here," Dion muttered under his breath.

"But we have to be," Ayana shot back, gripping the golden shard in her pocket. The warmth from it pulsed steadily, guiding her forward.

Lanelle reached out, fingers brushing against the ivy-covered stone wall. "If this Veil is guarding the path, then we need to prove we 'know' something."

"Know what?" Dion scowled.

Damien exhaled, scanning the walls. "The Garden's original name. Whatever was lost, whatever it was before."

Ayana stared at the door, at the way the vines trembled slightly, as if recognizing her presence. Then, without thinking, she whispered, "Eldoria's Veil."

A gust of wind burst from the entrance, sending leaves spiraling through the air. The vines recoiled, slithering back like living creatures. The massive stone door groaned before swinging open.

Lanelle whistled low. "Well, damn. How did you know that"

Damien squared his shoulders. "This is it. Where did you get that from?"

Ayana shrugged. "I don't know. I just, it just, I don't know it just came to me."

They stepped through the entrance and into a world far darker than they remembered. The Garden was sick, its once-lush grounds riddled with decay. Shadows moved where there should have been light. And at the core—at the very heart of its magic—something waited.

A shadowed beast erupted from the overgrown foliage, its jagged limbs twisting unnaturally as it let out a guttural screech. Damien yanked Ayana back, his arm bracing protectively in front of her.

Lanelle's fire ignited in her palm instantly. "I *knew* this wasn't going to be easy."

Dion clenched his fists, frost spreading up his arms. "Then let's get to work."

The creatures swarmed, their glowing eyes locking onto the intruders. The Garden's sickness had birthed abominations— twisted beings formed from shadows and decay. One pounced at Lanelle, but she spun, hurling a stream of fire straight into its chest. It shrieked as the flames consumed it, crumbling into ash.

Damien ducked low, slashing his blade through the tendrils of another beast before rolling to avoid a second strike. "We have to move forward! They're trying to keep us from the core!"

Ayana dodged a razor-sharp limb, gripping the golden shard tight. "Then we fight our way through."

Dion let loose a wave of ice, freezing one of the creatures in place before shattering it with a powerful kick. "Don't have to tell me twice."

Lanelle barely dodged a clawed limb, pivoting into a precise arc before releasing a pulse of energy that sent two creatures staggering. Dion followed up, ice lancing across the ground, freezing their feet before shattering them with a devastating kick.

More monsters emerged, twisted things with gaping maws and glistening black claws. Lanelle hurled another burst of flame, illuminating the battlefield, while Damien took down a creature with a well-placed dagger strike to its throat.

A monstrous, wolf-like creature lunged from the shadows, knocking Ayana to the ground. She gritted her teeth, raising her hands just as vines shot from the ground, wrapping around the beast and dragging it back. She didn't even have time to process it before she was on her feet again, heart hammering.

Then, as the final monster fell, a low rumbling shook the ground beneath them.

At the heart of the battlefield, a twisted, ancient statue began to move, its stone form cracking apart to reveal a hidden chamber beneath it.

The next clue awaited.

* * *

They stepped into the chamber, and the stench of decay hit them instantly. The Core—once the heart of The Garden's magic—was a withered husk of its former self. Vines, blackened and brittle, snaked across the walls, pulsing with an eerie, sickly light. The air was thick and heavy with something unnatural. It was as though the very essence of the place had been strangled, its breath stolen by the creeping darkness.

Damien grimaced. "It's worse than I imagined."

Ayana approached cautiously, her fingers grazing one of the shriveled vines. It crumbled to dust. "If we don't fix this, The Garden is done."

The ground beneath them was cracked. Roots curled in on themselves, rotting from the inside out. A sickly green mist clung to the air, swirling around their ankles, whispering in a ancient language.

At the center of the chamber, an ancient pedestal held a cracked stone tablet, its inscriptions barely legible. Ayana brushed away the dust, revealing the words:

Balance must be restored. The heart calls for its missing piece.

Dion exhaled sharply. "That's not cryptic at all."

They spread out, searching the chamber for clues. Lanelle inspected the brittle vines, tracing their decay with her fingertips. Damien examined the tablet, muttering old phrases from his grandfather's journals under his breath. Dion paced the edges of the room, kicking at the scattered rubble, looking for anything.

Ayana, however, felt something tugging at her, guiding her deeper into the chamber. She placed her palm against the wall, and a faint warmth spread up her arm. The stone beneath her fingers vibrated.

"There's something here," she murmured.

Damien hurried over, watching as Ayana pressed harder against the wall. "What is it?"

"I don't know, but it feels...alive."

Lanelle stepped back from the dying vines and crossed her arms. "Maybe the missing piece isn't a thing. Maybe it's energy. A source of life, like a key."

Dion let out a heavy sigh. "Fantastic. So where do we find an ancient magical key in a dying garden?"

A cold wind howled through the chamber. The shadows deepened, coiling together at the far end of the room. The unnatural darkness slithered forward, swallowing the faint glow of the decaying vines. The temperature plummeted, frost forming on the stone walls.

Then—he emerged.

The Shadow Figure.

The very presence sent a shiver through Ayana's bones. His form wavered, his silhouette more void than substance, his presence an absence, a hole in reality itself. Two glowing eyes of cold fire locked onto them with chilling intensity.

"You should not have come," the figure intoned, as if spoken by a thousand voices at once.

He moved with inhuman speed, striking before they could react. Tendrils of darkness lashed outward, snaring Lanelle and Dion first, hurling them backward like ragdolls. They hit the stone walls with bone-rattling force before crumpling to the ground, unconscious.

Damien barely had time to raise his blade before he was caught in the suffocating grasp of shadow and sent flying across the room. He groaned as he slumped against the far wall, unmoving.

Ayana stood alone.

The Shadow Figure loomed over her, taller than before, feeding off the corruption of the room. "You cannot stop this," he whispered. "This place belongs to me now."

Her pulse roared in her ears. The golden shard in her pocket burned like fire, and something deep inside her stirred. The veins on her arms glowed, pulsing with golden light, tracing intricate patterns beneath her skin, alive with raw energy. The

Garden's magic was calling to her.

Ayana clenched her fists. "You're wrong."

The Shadow Figure flicked his wrist, and a wave of darkness surged toward her. Ayana dodged, rolling to the side just as the energy struck the empty spot where she had stood, cracking the stone. She spun, extending her hands, and vines erupted from the earth, golden and pulsing with light. They shot toward the figure, twisting and binding, but he merely chuckled as they withered upon contact, turning to ash.

"You don't understand," he said, his voice crawling under her skin like ice. "This place is already dead. Its magic is mine now."

Ayana's breath came fast, but she didn't falter. "Then I'll bring it back."

She thrust her hands forward, and the very air around her shimmered. The golden light of her veins surged outward, crackling with energy. The vines beneath her feet pulsed, responding to her call, coiling and twisting, reinforcing the chamber against his corruption.

"Impossible," The Shadow Figure hissed.

Ayana advanced, each step forcing the darkness back. The room trembled as power surged through her, a connection forming between her and the wounded Core. She could feel its pain, its longing for balance, its desperation to be whole again.

And then, she understood.

The missing piece.

She had to return the shard.

Ayana lifted the golden fragment, pressing it against the Core. The moment it made contact, a shockwave of energy burst through the chamber, golden light surging outward in brilliant waves. The dying vines absorbed the energy, regaining their lost vitality as the Garden fought back.

The Shadow Figure let out an enraged shriek, lunging at her, but Ayana met him head-on. The golden energy exploded from her, a blinding wave of light that engulfed them both.

For a heartbeat, the world stood still.

Then the chamber shattered, magic pulsing outward in every direction. The corrupted vines caught fire with golden light, burning away the sickness, restoring the balance that had been lost.

When the dust settled, Ayana stood alone.

The Shadow Figure was gone.

The darkness had been driven out.

The Core pulsed, whole once more, its light strong and steady.

Ayana exhaled shakily, her body trembling. Her friends began to stir, groaning as they regained consciousness. Damien was the first to lift his head, his gaze locking onto her. "What... happened?"

She turned to them, exhaustion weighing her down.

"We won."

Well, That Escalated Quickly

Lanelle let out a heavy sigh and stretched. "Alright, so we saved The Garden. Now what?"

Dion shot her a side glance, rubbing the sore spot on his arm from where he had been thrown into a wall. "Now we deal with the unfinished business."

Damien wiped the sweat from his forehead, glancing toward the darkened sky. "We need to get back to campus before we raise suspicions." He turned to Ayana. "Are you okay to walk?"

Ayana nodded, exhausted. "Yeah. We should go."

Just then, Michael stepped into the Core's chamber, his presence causing a ripple in the newly restored magic. The air around him felt charged.

Lanelle and Dion exchanged a look. "Take us back," Lanelle said quickly. "Y'all can stay. We have things to take care of anyway."

Damien frowned. "You sure?"

Dion waved him off. "We just need to check on something first. Nothing major."

Damien gave them a long look but didn't press it. He opened the portal so Lanelle and Dion could go in, then he grabbed Ayana's hand and turned toward Michael.

"Did you feel it?" Damien asked as Michael approached.

"The Garden—it's whole again."

Michael nodded, his gaze unreadable. "The magic has been restored...and for that, I thank you."

Something unsettling tugging at the edge of Ayana's consciousness. His demeanor had changed—subtly, but unmistakably. A weight clung to his features, something old and sorrowful.

Then it hit her.

Her breath caught, and she took a step back. "No...no, it's you."

Michael's gaze darkened. "Ayana, let me explain."

Damien stiffened. "Explain what?"

"You're the Shadow Figure," Ayana said, voice barely above a whisper. "You poisoned The Garden."

Michael inhaled sharply. "Yes," he admitted. "But it's not as simple as it seems."

Damien's hand instinctively moved toward his blade. "Try us."

Michael held up his hands, making no move to defend himself. "I was once its guardian—one of many. The Garden's magic was ancient, powerful, and it called to those who could wield it. But power...it has a way of corrupting even the best of us." His expression twisted with pain. "I thought I was protecting it. I thought I could make it stronger, better. But in my arrogance, I opened a door that should have remained closed."

Ayana's hands clenched into fists. "You let the darkness in."

Michael nodded. "And once it took hold, it would not let go. I became something else. The shadows consumed me, turning me into the very thing I swore to fight against. I was no longer a guardian—I was its disease."

Damien's grip on his blade tightened. "You could have fought it."

Michael's voice broke. "I tried. I only had enough strength to ask for your help. But the darkness is patient. It whispers, it manipulates. By the time I realized what I had done, The Garden was already dying."

Ayana stared at him, searching for deception, but all she found was regret. "So why now?" she asked. "Why come back now?"

Michael exhaled shakily. "Because I felt it—when you restored the Core. When you brought back what I had destroyed. it freed me. The curse that bound me to the shadows was broken."

Damien narrowed his eyes. "And we're just supposed to believe that?"

Michael met his gaze evenly. "No. But you don't have to believe me. The Garden speaks for itself."

Ayana glanced around. The vines were now vibrant, the once-barren ground pulsing with renewed energy. The magic wasn't rejecting Michael. It was...accepting him.

She took a deep breath. "I don't know if I can forgive you for what you did."

Michael lowered his head. "I don't deserve your forgiveness."

"But," she continued, "I do believe in second chances."

Michael looked up, surprise flickering in his eyes. "You would trust me again?"

Ayana shook her head. "Trust? No. Not yet. But if The Garden is willing to give you another chance, then maybe..." She let out a breath. "Maybe we should too."

Michael's expression softened, and for the first time, there was something like hope in his eyes. "Then I will prove to you that I can still protect it. I will spend the rest of my days making up for what I've done."

Ayana held out her hand. After a long moment, Michael took it.

Damien exhaled heavily. "This is a mistake," he muttered. But when he looked at Ayana's unwavering resolve in her gaze, he sighed. "Fine. But I swear, if you even think about betraying us again—"

Michael nodded solemnly. "You have my word. I will not fail again."

A peaceful silence fell over them.

Ayana turned back to the glowing vines and the now-healed Core. "Let's go home."

Together, they stepped through the portal, leaving behind the shadows—but carrying forward the promise of something new.

* * *

As if summoned by their thoughts, a cold breeze swept through the trees. And then—she appeared.

The silver-haired girl stood at the edge of the space around them, her storm-gray eyes unreadable. Moonlight glowed against her pale skin, making her almost translucent against the night.

"You are persistent," she said, voice as soft as the rustling leaves. "That is good."

Lanelle crossed her arms. "You keep showing up like some tragic ghost. It's time for answers."

Dion took a step forward, his eyes narrowing. "Who are you? And what do you want?"

The girl studied them both for a long moment before speaking. "My name was—*is*—Elysia. And I was once like you... vessels."

"Vessels for what?"

Elysia hesitated before stepping closer, her movements unnervingly smooth. "Magic. You were never meant to wield it as you do. It was never yours to keep."

A sharp gust of wind rushed through the air around them, crackling faintly, as if responding to her words.

Lanelle tensed. "Oh, hell no."

Dion's jaw clenched. "What are you talking about?"

Elysia's gaze flicked to the now-dormant stone embedded within the roots. "The rock it was never a simple fragment of corruption. It was a siphon, a tool designed to extract magic. It takes...and it redistributes."

Realization dawned on Lanelle. "You were here to *take* from us."

"Your magic is powerful," Elysia tilted her head slightly, expression unreadable. Too powerful. I was sent to ensure it did not fall into the wrong hands."

Dion took a step back, instinctively raising his hands, ice sparking along his fingertips. "Sent by who?"

Elysia's lips curled into something almost like regret. "By those who watch from the shadows. By those who have long kept balance."

Lanelle's hands curled into fists, flames flickering at her fingertips. "So what? You were just gonna drain us dry?"

"I was meant to take what was never meant to be yours," Elysia sighed. "The balance must be maintained."

The wind howled suddenly, and the air around them crackled, flickered, turning dark for the briefest of moments before snapping back into its natural glow.

Lanelle's eyes darted to Dion. "Yeah, that sounds like some top-tier manipulation."

Dion nodded. "We're not letting that happen."

"You don't understand," Elysia's shoulders tensed.

"No," Dion said, voice firm. "You don't."

Elysia's fingers twitched as though she were hesitating. Then, her storm-gray eyes hardened. "Then you leave me no choice."

The stone at the heart of the roots pulsed violently, sending out a shockwave of energy. Lanelle and Dion staggered back as a force unlike anything they had felt before tore through the air. A brilliant explosion of magic erupted between them, sending splinters of light and shadow crashing outward. The ground trembled.

Dion barely had time to shield his face. A blinding white light enveloped the space, swallowing everything in its path. Lanelle's flames surged, colliding with the wave of power, and for a moment, time seemed to stretch, caught between forces too vast to contain.

Then—silence.

When the light faded, Elysia was gone.

The space around them lay in ruins. The stone was nowhere to be seen.

"What the hell just happened?" Dion looked around pushed himself to his feet, scanning for any trace of Elysia, but there was nothing. Just the eerie stillness of a place that had been changed forever.

Lanelle wiped a hand down her face. "We need to tell Mom."

Dion let out a breath, nodding. "Yeah. We really do."

Silently, they turned away from the ruined clearing, stepping back into the world that suddenly felt far more dangerous than before.

Also by Sheyanne Warren

Catch up on book one.

Spied: A Deceptive High Series

Dion and Lanelle are 14-year-old twins excited about the summer before high school. The most stressful thing on their plates are Lanelle figuring out which protective style to wear next and Dion keeping all of his girls straight. One night, their parents dropped a bomb on them. They have to trade in high school for boarding school. Even though Dion thinks it might be cool, Lanelle is convinced it is the end of the world.

Not only are they going to boarding school, but Douglas High is a high school for spies in training. And, it's the same high school their parents went to. Yes, their parents are spies!! Lanelle is too overwhelmed to think straight let alone maneuver this new world she's been thrown into. Dion is trying to find his footing and always seems to get into trouble. With new powers come new enemies and a whole new set of rules. Will the twins survive life at Deceptive High?